WOMAN
VANISHES

ALSO BY CAROLINE CRANE

WOMAN VANISHES

Caroline Crane

DODD, MEAD & COMPANY
New York

Published by Dodd, Mead & Company, Inc.
79 Madison Avenue, New York, N.Y. 10016
Distributed in Canada by
McClelland and Stewart Limited, Toronto
Manufactured in the United States of America

First Edition

Library of Congress Cataloging in Publication Data

Crane, Caroline.
    Woman vanishes.

    I. Title.
PS3553.R2695W6   1984   811'.54   83-20835
ISBN 0-396-08310-2

For Laurel

WOMAN
VANISHES

1

"That's it?" Jarvis asked. "Five percent?"

The big man settled back in the cramped confines of the diner booth. He stirred his coffee delicately, with his pinkie finger arched above the spoon. His fingers were pudgy and soft, shapeless, like sausages. He wore an array of heavy rings. Between the two hands, Jarvis estimated, there must have been six to eight rings.

The man's face perspired in the late May warmth. In spite of the informality of the diner, he kept on his jacket. It was made of a rich-looking silky material, a dark silver-blue. His hair was black, graying at the temples. That, too, looked silver.

Because the man kept his jacket on, Jarvis did too. Jarvis had come to him begging, but he couldn't feel inferior. His blond, establishment looks spoke of long-standing money. Of family and privilege. He had simply fallen on hard times.

"Five percent a week," said the man. Jarvis didn't know his name. He called himself "the Broker."

Jarvis said, "That's less than a bank, isn't it?"

"I don't know about banks," replied the Broker. "I'm in business for myself. How much are you looking for?"

"I was thinking—I know it's a lot. I could use thirty, maybe forty thousand, but that's just what I could use. Anything would help. I have a house in Allenbury that's worth more than that, but I'm not in a position to sell it right now. I could offer it as collateral, though. And my business, of course, but that's—" He gave a soundless chuckle. "That's why I'm here. It's not in the greatest shape. I also," he added, "have a boat and two cars."

With a flap of his hand, the Broker dismissed the boat and two cars. Even the house and the business.

"I don't need collateral," he said. "You're the only collateral I need. You want the money, you pay me interest every week. That's the way I do business. Every week I'll collect. On a forty-thousand-dollar loan, that'll be two thousand a week."

"Two thousand a week?"

"That's what I said."

Two thousand. Jarvis felt a clutching in his chest. Two thousand was a hell of a lot. But if he started with forty, he could use it sparingly and begin paying from that.

The truth was, he hadn't much choice. The Broker was his last chance to save the business, and therefore himself.

"Okay," he said. "Where do I sign?"

The Broker's thick lips widened in a smile.

"You don't sign. It's two thousand a week. I don't need a piece of paper. I'll remember it. So will you."

2

It was sometime around the end of May, Pauline remembered, that Jarvis had told her their troubles were over. She assumed he was talking about the job he had found. It was part-time, selling and installing air conditioners for a not-very-generous commission, but it was something they could rely on, unlike that shaky little publishing business he had founded. Besides, she was not very keen on his publishing erotica, even though he insisted it was "high-class stuff."

For a while after he started the new job, he had seemed on top of the world. At last it began to look as though they might make it.

But the mood had not stayed with him. Things weren't working out after all, and his old depression returned. He talked of selling the boat and one of the cars. Before that, he had insisted upon keeping his membership in the yacht club even when they could no longer afford it. He needed the contacts, he said. "It's people like that who can help me get the kind of job I want."

3

Yet the longer he went without a job, the harder it was to find one. Nobody liked a loser. And the publishing venture only drained away money instead of earning it. He would be coming home soon. She looked out of the window, watching for his car on the driveway. He had worked late that night. July had begun with a blast of hot, muggy weather, and all the people who thought they could live without air conditioning suddenly decided they couldn't.

Still, he must have made good money, working a twelve-hour day. It was almost nine o'clock, and Saturday, too. In the old days, on Saturday evenings, they would have been dining out, or seeing a show at the summer playhouse. Or going to a party, or giving one. Or, at the very least, relaxing around the pool after a dinner of thick barbecued steak.

She set the table in the breakfast nook with a light supper of tuna salad and buttered toast. Since Kirby was already asleep, it would be just the two of them, a special, intimate time together.

Even at night the kitchen was a pleasant haven, although it was at its best in the morning. Then the sun shone in through flocked curtains, lighting the room that always reminded her of daisies, yellow and white and airy, with the breakfast nook set off from the rest by a divider of white latticework.

She remembered the day the decorators had finished. It was an unforgettable day, and not because of the decorators. She remembered her delight in having a whole new kitchen filled with new, efficient appliances, with a built-in microwave oven and wallpaper that picked up the latticework motif. She felt it was really her home at

4

last. All the old things that her mother-in-law had used were gone.

But when she called Jarvis at his office in New York to tell him the work was finished, he was silent for a moment. Then he said, "Don't pay them."

He would not explain over the phone. Only when he arrived home in the evening did she learn what had happened. That day, the same day the expensive decorating job was finished, Thomas & Flute, the book publishers, had told him they were letting him go.

It was not his fault. They made that clear. It was because of the merger with Hyram House and a subsequent cutback of duplicate staff.

At the time, she thought Jarvis was too pessimistic about it, that he was suffering from shock. But fourteen months had justified his initial pessimism. Fourteen months later he still didn't have a real job, and his own attempt at publishing was falling on its face.

She saw the lights of his car as he turned into the driveway. Heard the garage door open and the roar of his engine, then heard it switched off.

His footsteps in the entryway sounded slow and tired. He came into the kitchen carrying a long, lumpy package wrapped in green florist's paper.

Oh, no, she thought.

He held out the package. "For you. Because I love you."

"Oh, Jarvis," She took the flowers from him and removed the wrapping. Dark red, long-stemmed roses. There must have been a dozen.

"Jarvis . . . "

He smiled, and some of the fatigue left his face.

5

"I always wanted to get those for you," he said. "They're like you. The same dark, vivid coloring—except you're not red. And long stems."

"But we—"

There were so many things they needed more than roses. They still owed on last winter's fuel bill. If they didn't pay it soon, they would get no fuel in the coming winter.

"Thank you, Jarvis. That was sweet."

She refrained from saying anything else. Anything that began with "but" or "why." You couldn't do that to Jarvis.

"I'll put them in water." She turned her back to reach a vase from the cupboard, so he could not see her clench her teeth in despair.

Finally she could speak again. "What's the occasion?"

"Nothing in particular. It's just that I've put you through a lot, I know. This is kind of to make up for it."

"Oh ... well ... They're beautiful." She filled the vase with warm water and cut the stems at an angle to make the flowers last.

"I fixed a cold supper," she said, "because of the weather. Sit down and I'll tell you about an idea I had."

"I can't eat in these clothes. I stink." He went upstairs to change. Probably he would take a shower. Jarvis was so fastidious. She could not get used to seeing him in work clothes. Not her Jarvis, with his direct blue gaze and square, go-getter jaw that seemed to get him nothing. He had a clean, polished look. An urban look. He belonged in a three-piece suit.

She was right, he did take a shower. He came downstairs in clean clothes and smelling of Irish Spring soap.

6

He sat down at the table and stared at his plate. She set a glass of iced water in front of him and helped herself to salad.

"Now do you want to hear my plan?" she asked. "Remember you told me it would be silly if I went out to work, because then you'd have to stay home and babysit instead of looking for a job? Well, I got to thinking it would be just perfect if I could run a business right here in the house."

He looked at her in surprise. "We already have a business."

"You don't mean Venus Press."

"Why don't I?"

"Well, I'd sort of like to make a new start with something different. I thought I'd try to find something that wouldn't cost too much to get going. Maybe some kind of mail order business. I could begin very small and just advertise locally until I started to make some money. Jarvis, are you listening?"

She could see by his eyes that he had tuned her out and drifted elsewhere. With some effort he managed to come back.

He said, "Do you mind if we don't talk about it right now?"

"Why? What's the matter?"

He wasn't eating. He had picked up his fork, put it into the salad, and then stopped.

"Is something wrong?" she asked. "Do you want to tell me about it?"

"No, not really." He poked at a slice of hard-boiled egg.

"If something's on your mind, I wish you'd share it with me. Aren't we in this together?"

"Maybe, but not all of it."

"It doesn't have to be that way, Jarvis. I keep telling you I want to work and help out, and this way I could do it without making any more problems for you. I saw an article in a magazine—"

His muscles tensed. "Knock it off, okay?"

"Okay, but please understand that I only want to help. We're partners, remember? It isn't your problem alone."

He set down his fork. "I'm sorry. I didn't mean to yell."

"You didn't."

"I didn't?"

"Yell."

"That's good, because I didn't mean to. But Paulie, we've been over this whole thing a dozen times."

"What whole thing? This is different. Did you hear anything I said?"

"I really don't want to talk about it now."

"Tomorrow?"

He did not reply. She knew he was under a strain, but this was something that affected both of them, their life together, and their child. And it could not be put off indefinitely.

"Jarvis," she said, "I realize you're tired, but at least you can listen. I have a stake in this, too. I want to do my part, and I want to know what's going on."

"Nothing's going on, okay?" He stood up from the table. "I already told you, it's nothing."

Pauline stood up, too. "It must be something. You're not letting me in on things. Like those job interviews you said you were having in Yonkers."

Did she imagine that he turned a little pale?

"What kind of job," she went on, "would make you go

8

for an interview every Thursday, week after week? Is that another of your schemes?"

"Pauline—" His tone warned her.

"Why is it such a big secret? You won't tell me anything. Is it the CIA? Are you applying for the CIA?"

"You just won't let up, will you? I'm going in the den." He opened the refrigerator. "Where's the beer? Don't we have any beer?"

"I thought you might have noticed," she said, "that we're a little broke these days, and beer is a luxury item."

"I need something cold, and don't tell me to drink water. It looks as if I'll have to take care of it myself." He started out toward the garage.

"You didn't eat your dinner," she reminded him.

"I don't feel like eating." Slowly he came back to her. He glanced toward the roses, still on the counter in their glass vase. She was wrenched, thinking of what they stood for. He had tried, the only way he knew how. He was a romantic. She had never really defined it before. With Jarvis, romanticism was almost a disability.

He took her in his arms and together they rocked gently, back and forth.

"I love you, Pauline," he said.

"I love you, too, even if you're crazy."

"I am?"

"You know you are. Hopelessly impractical. Maybe that's one reason why I love you. It's an attraction of opposites."

"I don't know if I believe in that, but it seems to work for us," he said. "I'll see you later. Take care."

3

They had quarreled last night. Pauline woke, remembering. It was not really a quarrel, just words. It had something to do with money.

The room was hot and bright. She closed her eyes again and luxuriated in the fact that it was Sunday. And summer. There would be no rushing to get Kirby off to nursery school or Jarvis to the 7:23. That was the only good thing about their present situation.

Still half asleep, she reached across the bed. Her hand touched air. She turned and stared at the empty mattress.

Maybe he was in the bathroom. She listened, but the only sound came from a mourning dove somewhere in the garden. It was only seven o'clock. At seven on Sundays, he was usually asleep.

Maybe downstairs. She listened for kitchen noises. He had to be somewhere. But she could not stop thinking about the argument they had had.

It was her fault. Stupid of her. She should have remembered how a man's ego was bound up with his income. In spite of her good intentions, she had obviously hit a nerve.

Afterward he had gone out to buy beer. He was out for a long time. Probably went to visit somebody, or maybe to a bar. She did remember his coming back. She had been in bed, but not asleep. He had said something to her. An apology of sorts. Later she heard him bustling around in the dark. Back and forth, in and out of the room. She could not imagine what he was doing. Getting ready to sleep in the guest room, most likely, because she had made him angry.

She sat up, letting the sheet fall away from her damp body. Now she could feel the breeze that fluffed out the curtains. It was a whisper on her bare skin. She went into the bathroom, brushed her teeth, and took a quick shower. She left the door open, but he didn't come. He must have heard the shower. Probably he was still annoyed with her. His situation made him touchy. She sprinkled herself with baby powder, slipped into a cotton duster, and started down the hall.

The door to Kirby's room was open, as Pauline had left it, for ventilation. Kirby lay asleep, one hand tangled in her red-gold hair, the other thumb in her mouth. Four years old, and still she sucked her thumb when she was sleeping. A sign of insecurity, one of Pauline's friends had said. The pediatrician assured her that it was nothing to worry about.

She reached the guest room and looked inside. It was empty. Both beds were made up and undisturbed.

He would have slept there if he had been anywhere. No one would choose a couch downstairs when he could

11

have a comfortable bed. Not even an angry Jarvis. Unless he had cheated on their agreement to save electricity, and slept in the den with the air conditioner on. She went downstairs to look.

He was not in the den. Or the living room, the patio, or the kitchen. The only trace of him was an empty coffee cup in the kitchen sink.

That was it. He had gotten up early. She was surprised that she hadn't heard him. She went out the back door, across the patio and the still-damp grass, to a building that had once housed horses but was now the headquarters for Venus Press with its staff of one.

The door would not open. She tried it again, thinking it might be stuck. It was locked. She peered through a window into semidarkness.

"Jarvis?" she called, rapping on the window. There was no answer.

A prickly feeling crawled down her spine. If he was not here, and not in the house, where was he?

She returned to the house. He might be on the terrace.

The front door was locked. She opened it and looked out at the dewy expanse of lawn, the heavy humidity like a gray veil against the shrubbery. The empty terrace. And she remembered that when she went through the back door, it, too, had been locked.

He *had* come back last night after the beer. She hadn't dreamed it. Could he have gotten a job and started work this morning, Sunday morning, without telling her? Not likely. They would have been celebrating last night instead of bickering. He certainly would have told her. She picked up the newspaper from the front step and went

12

back inside.

She checked the garage. His car was gone.

She had known it would be. She wanted to think he had gotten up and perhaps driven into the village for reasons of his own, but she could not deny the evidence. That stain of coffee in the dirty cup was dry. And the newspaper on the front step—he would have brought it in and maybe looked at it for a while. He had gone before it was delivered. Sometime during the night. Gone out and had an accident. Or spent the night with someone.

"Mommy?"

"I'm down here, Kirby. In the kitchen."

A piece of paper caught her eye. A folded sheet of notepaper on the counter next to the coffeepot.

Dear Paulie. I'm sorry to do this to you, but I have no choice. It's better if you don't know anything about it. Please, please, do not try to find me. I mean that with all my heart. Give Kirby a hug for me, and both of you get on with your lives as best you can.

Clipped to the note were five twenty-dollar bills.

He had killed himself. She felt a rush of shock and then despair.

What am I going to do?

Kirby appeared in the kitchen doorway, trailing her pink blanket.

"Mommy, where's my daddy?"

"I don't know, baby. I think he went out somewhere with the car."

Was it that bad a quarrel? Had she been that terrible?

13

She ought to have known how on edge he was, unemployed for fourteen months and with his little business failing. It did terrible things to a person.

She read the note again. The second time, it did not sound as final. It was more as though he was running away from all the pressure.

Or maybe running *to* something. Maybe a woman. He couldn't do that to her. Could he?

"Can I have puffed rice?"

She needed coffee. Needed to think. Or maybe what she needed was a good stiff shot of something. She poured the cereal for Kirby and pushed it toward her.

"Can I have a spoon?" Kirby asked.

Pauline got out the spoon. "I'm sorry, baby. I'm not with it this morning."

"I'm not a baby."

"I know. That's just a pet name."

She looked again at the note, spread out on the counter. And the money. A hundred dollars. Was he serious? How long was that supposed to last her?

The pain and shock gave way to anger. *Damn you. Damn you, Jarvis, what am I going to do?*

If this past year had been hard for him, it was hard for her, too. Did he think it was all her fault? She had offered to go to work, many times. He had said she couldn't earn enough to make it worthwhile, but it would have helped. They were in this together. Until now.

Oh damn, she thought as reality struck her. *Now I'll have to get a job. This minute.*

Except that it was Sunday. And besides, there was Kirby to look after. What would she do?

14

It had been difficult, no doubt about it. But she could endure it all, the debts, the uncertainty, as long as he was with her, the two of them in it together. But now he had gone. Cracked under the strain. If he hadn't cracked, he would never have left her to face it alone.

"Mommy, can I have some orange juice?"

Pauline looked in the refrigerator. There was no juice made up. She opened a can and mixed it with tap water, which never ran cold in the summertime. Kirby asked for ice cubes.

"Not this time, sweetheart. I just can't deal with it."

They would have to change their whole way of life. "Get on with your lives," he had said. How did he expect her to do that?

She waited, screaming inside, while Kirby finished her breakfast. Then she went upstairs and looked through Jarvis's wardrobe to see what was missing.

She could not remember everything he owned, but he had taken all his underwear, most of his sports clothes, two suits, as far as she could tell, and his dark blue windbreaker. All that while she had slept. He had gone in and out of the bedroom, and she never knew what he was doing.

She stood back from the closet, feeling a hollowness that would not go away.

He couldn't have.

But evidently, he had. Still, with a last faint hope, she sat down at the telephone and dialed the number for Venus Press. She could almost hear it ringing back there in the stable. She could almost hear it stop when she hung up.

"Kirby, get your clothes on," she said.

15

"Why?"

She did not know quite why. It only seemed that, in this kind of emergency, they ought to be dressed. She could face it better if she were dressed. She got out a pair of freshly ironed shorts for herself and an aquamarine playsuit for Kirby. Pauline was tall and slender, with long dark hair and a deep summer tan. In her well-cut khaki shorts and white T-shirt, she still looked the young, well-to-do suburban matron, even though she was no longer well-to-do.

Taking a key this time, she and Kirby went back to the stable and unlocked the door.

"Where's Daddy?" Kirby asked.

"That's what I'd like to know."

The stalls had been removed and the stable divided into two long, low rooms. The smaller one, furnished with a battered steel desk and a file cabinet, was the editorial office. In the larger one, cartons of unsold books were stacked against one wall. The rest was empty and there were cobwebs in the corners. She searched for clues, anything that might suggest where he had gone, or why.

His files were all still in place, and so were his address lists. His desk was tidy, the way he always left it, with wire baskets of unanswered correspondence and unpaid bills.

And of course the books.

"Erotica is what sells," he had insisted when Pauline questioned his editorial taste. "Well-written erotica can be a beautiful thing. Look at Anais Nin."

She had never read Anais Nin. Had never particularly wanted to, and wasn't sure she would think it was beauti-

16

ful even if she did read it, but she couldn't argue with Jarvis. And she must never, never make the mistake of calling it pornography.

"It's hot in here," Kirby said.

"You're right. Let's go." She ushered Kirby out and locked the door. The stable reminded her of Pompeii. An everyday moment frozen in time, with the people gone forever.

Back in the kitchen, she made herself another cup of coffee. She would have to keep going. Try to think of something.

Her parents would help her, if she could find them. Since her father's retirement a year ago, they had had no permanent address. They traveled about in a motor home, stopping when and where they pleased. The last place had been a campground in Florida. They had raved about the palm-shaded cove, the sandy beaches. "Love it if you and Kirby could come for a visit." But she had chosen to stay with Jarvis. That was ironic now. She found their letter with the address and dialed Information.

When she reached the campground office, she was told that her parents had checked out and left no forwarding address.

She hung up the phone and sat, feeling paralyzed. There was no other place to turn. Eventually they would resettle and write to her again, but in the meantime, she and Kirby had to live.

She tried to shake off the paralysis. If only Jarvis would come back. But she couldn't go on thinking that way. She had only herself. And that was what paralyzed her.

Kirby came into the bedroom, where Pauline sat by

17

the phone. "Who were you talking to? Was it my daddy?"

Pauline looked at her daughter and wondered how much she could shield her from all that had happened.

"No, that wasn't Daddy, but I just had an idea."

Art Richards. He was Jarvis's employer, the man who owned the air-conditioning business. The man who had had none of Jarvis's advantages, but who made a nice profit while Jarvis was getting further into debt every day.

Since it was Sunday, the office would be closed. She dialed Art's home number before she stopped to remember how early it still was.

"What was that?" Art said when she explained her reason for disturbing him. "He's gone? What do you mean, gone?"

"I was hoping you might know something. He—" She was a deserted wife, and might as well admit it. "He was gone when I got up this morning. He took his clothes and left a note. He said I shouldn't try to find him."

"Do you think he might have—" Art dropped his voice.

"That's what I thought at first, but he wouldn't have taken his clothes. I guess he just couldn't handle any more, but I really thought he had more guts than that." She felt a small sense of vengeful satisfaction in making a point of Jarvis's gutlessness.

"Well, thanks for letting me know," Art said. "I was counting on him for tomorrow. We've got a lot of work lined up."

"Yes, I'm sorry. I just thought you might know something, and I was wondering if—if he might have any money coming to him."

"No, we're all settled up as of last night. Payday is Sat-

18

urday, you know."

"Yes, I know. Mr. Richards, I don't know what to do. He left me with just a hundred dollars, and I have a child to support. You said you were counting on him. Could I do the work?"

There was a startled pause and then a deep chuckle. "I don't think so, dear. We're dealing with big, heavy machines."

"How about your office? Could I work in your office?"

"Sorry again. The missus and I take care of that. Maybe you should try the county, especially if you've got a little kid."

"Maybe I should," Pauline said, and hung up. She hadn't thought of public assistance. Probably she wouldn't even qualify, when she had all this. The house and all. But what good was it? She couldn't sell it. Everything was in his name.

Once, in desperation, she had broached the idea of selling it.

"I know it's a treasure," she had said, "but with all the money we'd get for it, we could move into a cheap apartment and have enough to live on and pay our debts, too."

He would not even consider it. A treasure it certainly was, he said, and worth more to him in sentiment than in money. It was an old Colonial farmhouse, and had been in his family for three generations. It was the home in which he had grown up. The bathrooms had been added, the kitchen modernized, and his parents had put in the terraces and swimming pool.

"Besides," he had pointed out in an effort to add practicality to his sentiment, "once we sell it, it's gone. But if we can manage to hang onto it, then when our finances pick up, which they'll have to do sooner or later, we

19

won't have lost anything."

She thought they were already losing everything into the vast maw of Venus Press. The debts piled up unbelievably. Soon they would have to declare bankruptcy. By giving up the house and some of their other trappings, not to mention Venus Press, they could keep themselves afloat.

His note had implied that he would not be coming back. Part of her mind was busy planning how she would live without him, while another part could not accept it at all. If things had been that bad between them, wouldn't she have known? He had been angry and upset, but he would soon realize what he had done to her and come back, or at least telephone. She waited all day for some kind of message. Or better yet, the sound of his car. Until Monday, there was not much else she could do.

After Kirby went to bed that night, the house seemed cavernous. She locked the downstairs doors and sat on the bed with the television on to fill the silence. Far in the distance, thunder rumbled. And a doorbell rang.

She thought it came from the television. But the scene was set outdoors, a desert. She hadn't even noticed that she was watching a Western.

It must have been downstairs. She had locked the screen door. Jarvis would have to ring to get in. It was Jarvis! With a little cry of excitement, she jumped from her bed and ran downstairs.

Two strange men waited on the doorstep.

He's dead, she thought. *They've come to tell me he's dead.*

20

She opened the main door but kept the screen door locked. They were somber. Funereal, in dark suits. One man was heavyset, the other slender and bald, but with a smooth, young face.

"Mrs. Kingsley?" asked the heavy one.

"Yes?"

"We'd like to talk to you. How about letting us in?"

Maybe they were lawyers. Or detectives.

"Could you tell me what this is about?" she asked.

"It's about your husband. It's important. We can't talk out here."

They were lawyers. He wanted a divorce. Or maybe they were the FBI and he was in trouble. As she opened the door, she noticed a long black car parked out at the curb. Again she thought of funerals.

As soon as they were inside, the heavyset man closed and locked the door. "Tell me, Mrs. Kingsley, is your husband at home?"

"No, he's not." At least they hadn't come to tell her he was dead.

"When do you expect him?"

"I don't. I don't know if he's ever coming back."

"What do you mean by that?"

She stared at the man, not liking his tone and wishing she hadn't let him in.

"It means—" She tried to swallow. "It means he's gone. He was gone when I got up this morning. He took his clothes. Look, I don't even know who you are. Would you please explain what you want with my husband?"

"Don't you know that your husband borrowed some money?"

"I know he tried. From a bank. He was out of work."

21

The picture began to take shape. She could not yet put it into words. It wasn't true. This couldn't be happening.

The fat man took her elbow and led her toward the living room. "We can make ourselves comfortable while we talk this over." To the lanky one, he said, "You go take a look around. See if he's anywhere in the house."

"You can't search my house!" Pauline cried as the thin man started upstairs. The other man's grip tightened on her arm. She turned to him, screaming, "He's not here, I told you he's not! I have a child sleeping upstairs. You can't do this!"

The man found the dimmer switch and turned on the living room lights. He pushed Pauline toward the sofa. She sat down on the arm, lightly, ready to get up again if she could.

"You might as well relax, Mrs. Kingsley," he said. "We have a lot to talk about. It looks as if your husband didn't tell you very much, so I'm going to have to explain it myself."

The sofa arm was uncomfortable. She slid down into the cushions. Smiling pleasantly, the fat man seated himself in a chair opposite her.

"It's like this, Mrs. Kingsley," he began as he settled back in the chair and crossed his ankles. "Your husband, as I was starting to tell you, borrowed some money from a friend of mine. Forty thousand dollars, to be exact."

Her mouth opened.

"It was a deal," he said. "An agreement. Your husband was a willing party to it. He gets the loan, he agrees to pay a certain amount every week. Now my friend tells me he defaulted on the last couple of payments. We

22

don't do business that way, Mrs. Kingsley. We expect all parties to stick to the agreement."

"But he's not here. I told you that." She had an odd sense of unreality. In a little while they would go away, and it would be as though they had never come.

"The fact remains," said the man, "we expect those payments to be made. We're not a charity, Mrs. Kingsley, we're a business like any other business. Your husband understood the terms. He knew he was borrowing forty thousand dollars at five percent a week."

"Five percent?" It seemed very reasonable, considering the usual rate on a loan. Maybe it was a good thing that the bank had turned him down.

"Five percent a week," the man repeated. "Those are the terms your husband agreed to. Five percent interest a week comes to two hundred sixty a year, if you remember your arithmetic."

Bewildered, she echoed softly, "Two hundred sixty—"

"Percent, Mrs. Kingsley. Percent."

He was wrong. She couldn't remember her arithmetic, at least not in her head, but two hundred sixty percent a year was staggering. It would come to much more than he had borrowed. Almost three times as much.

"Is that legal?" she asked. "That kind of interest?"

The man folded his arms. "It's fairly standard in our business. Some go a lot higher. Your husband made the first three payments. Two thousand a week. That was the interest. Two grand a week. You pay the interest as long as the principal remains. If you get a little extra now and then, you pay back some of the principal."

"But that's slavery!" she cried as his face blurred. "Two thousand a week! He couldn't have known that. Are you

23

serious? Is he crazy?"

"I'm afraid insanity is no defense, Mrs. Kingsley. Those were the terms."

The thin man came in from the dining room. He shrugged his shoulders and held out empty hands.

"Looks like you're right, honey," said the fat man, "and that's why we're talking to you. The agreement was made and the money is going to be paid back, one way or another."

She tried to speak, but her throat was dry and she couldn't think what to say.

"Yes, Mrs. Kingsley, I mean you. It's up to you now, dear."

"But that's ridiculous! I don't have any money."

"We know you aren't employed. We know a lot about you, dear. But you could make some pretty good money, an attractive woman like you." His eyes traveled down her long, tanned legs to her bare feet. He turned to his companion. "Am I right?"

The thin man nodded in agreement.

"No way!" exclaimed Pauline. They heard the fear in her voice. Again the fat man smiled.

"You think of a better way, honey. You could bring in two, three hundred a day. Maybe more. I'll even make it easy for you. I'll send you the men. You won't have to go out and hustle. I know a lot of men who'd go for a classy chick like you."

"You're serious, aren't you?" She was numb. "You really think you could make me do something like that."

"I don't see where you've got any choice."

"But I have a little child. I can't—"

"You're a responsible mother, I can see that. You want

24

to be sure nothing happens to your child."

"Oh, my God."

"You never can tell what might happen to a kid. She's outside playing with her friends, maybe she gets lost, or hit by a car. Maybe an old well in somebody's backyard."

No. Not Kirby. No.

"You're threatening my child. You wouldn't hurt a child just for money. It's not her fault."

The fat man started out toward the entryway. "Nobody's threatening your kid, Mrs. Kingsley. We're talking about some of the things that can happen. It's not easy to keep a kid safe these days."

For the first time, the thin man spoke. "There's perverts, too. You never can tell."

"Even you could get hurt," added the fat man. "You drive a car, you have a swimming pool out back. And I've heard of people being trapped when the house catches fire."

They were leaving. She ran after them. "My husband left me a hundred dollars. I can give it to you now. Will that help?"

The fat man pretended to count on his fingers. "Let's see, there's the last two weeks, and this week coming up. Payment's due on Thursday, by the way. Every Thursday. That's six grand total through this week. Less a hundred makes five grand nine hundred. Where's the five grand nine hundred going to come from, Mrs. Kingsley?"

They meant it. Absolutely. Six thousand dollars. There was no escape.

"Where can I get in touch with you?" She felt as though someone were speaking for her.

25

"You can't get in touch with us. We'll be in touch with you. Think you can come up with six grand?"

"I'll try."

She saw their swift appraisal of her home. She couldn't tell them it was in his name. Let them think she had a chance of getting the money.

"Give me a couple of days?" she asked.

The fat man rested his hand on the door. "That's just through this week, remember. Don't forget the week after, and the one after that. And don't try anything cute, like leaving town. We'll be keeping an eye on you, baby."

She watched them go down the walk toward the parked car, then watched the car glide away. Outside the screen door, a soft rain was falling. The air smelled of damp earth and leaves. She locked both doors and went upstairs.

4

She stood by the window in the guest room, watching the road. In her mind, the conversation played itself over and over again.

It's up to you now, dear.

Two thousand a week. For as long as the principal remains.

You never know what can happen to a kid.

She might have thought they were bluffing, except for Jarvis. *He* hadn't thought they were bluffing. And he was in a position to know.

She went to her own room, picked up the telephone and dialed the police.

"Hello? I'm out on Dogwood Road. Two men were just here. They wanted money. They said they were going to kill my child."

"Where is your child now?"

"Oh, she's here. She's asleep. They just said—they said my husband owes them money."

"Your name and address?"

27

"Oh—yes. Pauline Kingsley. It's—" She could not remember her address. "One forty-nine Dogwood Road."

"We'll send a man right over, Mrs. Kingsley."

She closed her eyes and leaned back on her bed. She could not believe it had happened. Not to her. It was some kind of dream. Jarvis would never do a thing like that.

But he might, not knowing what he was getting into. Because he was Jarvis. Or he might somehow delude himself that it would all work out. And he wouldn't want her to know about it. Yes, Jarvis could do that.

I'll even send you the men. You wouldn't have to hustle.

She roused herself and went downstairs to wait by the door. After ten minutes, a police car arrived. A uniformed patrolman stepped out and identified himself. His name was Robert Alwood. She unlocked the screen door.

"I'm so glad you're here," she said. "I wish you didn't ever have to leave."

She led him into the living room and told him about the visit from the two men.

"They said he borrowed forty thousand dollars. I didn't even know about it. And I can't pay it. As it is, I don't have enough to live on. They wanted two thousand a week. There's no way I can get that kind of money," she emphasized as he studied the well-furnished room.

"My husband lost his job over a year ago. He couldn't get another one, so he tried to start a business of his own, but all it did was lose money. He kept trying to revive it with more money. Now he's gone. I have exactly a hundred dollars that he left me, and no income. They want two thousand a *week*. And that's only interest."

28

"It's a typical loan shark deal," said the policeman.

"You mean those things really happen?"

"All the time, ma'am."

"What do people do?"

"They pay. If they can. Or they go to the authorities, like you did. Or sometimes they get beaten up, or—I'd better not say it."

"But is it legal, that kind of interest?"

"No, it's not."

"Then how can they do it? They were so out in the open about the whole thing."

"Were they? Did they give you their names?"

"No."

"Phone number? Address? Did they hand you a business card, like a legitimate person would?"

"No, they said I couldn't get in touch with them. They'd be in touch with me."

"Think about it. That's not out in the open. They came in the night, got away fast, and they didn't tell you anything that could point to who they were."

"I could give you a description. Both of them."

"I'd better explain something to you, ma'am. What we have here is an account of two men coming to your house and trying to collect a debt. We don't have any actual proof of a crime being committed."

"You said it was illegal."

"Right, it is. But the way the law works, there's not much we can do without some proof—and I mean proof that will stand up in a court of law—that a crime was actually committed."

"You mean you can't do anything? But he threatened my child! What do I have to do, wait till she gets hit by a car? Will that be proof?"

"Ma'am, I want you to understand what we're up against. These men are professionals. They know how to cover their tracks. Chances are, there isn't even a traceable record of the transaction."

"Then how can they enforce it?"

He was a young man with an earnest face and round eyes that regarded her owlishly.

"You must know they've got their ways," he said. "Isn't that why you called me here?"

"Yes. They came to intimidate me. It would have worked, too, if I had the money. I'd pay anything to keep my child safe."

And go on paying forever? That was how the arrangement had sounded.

"Wait a minute," she said, "he kept talking about my husband signing an agreement. Wouldn't that be some kind of proof?"

"He did say that?"

"No ... no, I'm sorry, he didn't say 'sign.' He said 'agreed to.' That was it. My husband agreed to the terms. But he couldn't have known what he was doing. And I don't understand them charging an interest like that. How do they expect people to pay it?"

"That's the crux of their operation," Alwood explained. "That kind of interest, they call it 'vigorish,' or 'juice.' That's how they make their money. You see, what usually happens is the big boss might give each of his top men a certain sum of money, maybe a hundred thousand each, and says he wants it back in a year with one percent interest, something like that. Then each of them will spread it around to the guys under them, and so on.

30

Naturally they have to increase the interest rate so each man gets his cut. And they have to make sure they collect, because the boss doesn't settle for empty promises. The whole thing is strictly illegal, but it's almost impossible to prove anything against them."

She listened, and it still seemed unreal. It couldn't be happening to her.

"Then I guess they really mean it," she said.

"You can bet on that."

"What am I supposed to do?"

"Like I told you before, ma'am, what we really need is proof."

"What proof? You said they cover their own tracks. Oh, but look, my husband ran away. That shows that something happened, anyway. And he left a note."

She went to the dining room, where she had tucked the note among Jarvis's long-stemmed roses. Alwood looked at it briefly, then handed it back to her.

"Yes, I see, but it's not really evidence of anything. He doesn't tell you what happened. Even if he did, it wouldn't stand up to a defense attorney."

"Then what am I supposed to do?" she cried. "I'm not asking to get them prosecuted. All I want is some protection for myself and my child. Why is that so difficult?"

"I understand how you feel, believe me," he said. "Unfortunately, we're not a large force. We just don't have the manpower for guard service. But wait, ma'am, I'm not finished. I was going to say, if you're willing to cooperate with us, we can work together and try to put that whole operation out of business."

She did not like the sound of it. Warily she asked, "What do you mean?"

31

"Well, I can't work out the details with you myself, but I can tell you basically how it's done. Next time they contact you, you'd agree to meet with them. Then you let us know, or whatever authorities you're working with on it. They'd fix you up with an invisible microphone and tape recorder, so we can get a record of the whole conversation. That way, you see, there'd be some concrete proof of what's going on. Of the intimidation and extortion part, anyway. We get a lot of valuable information that way. And then we take it from there."

"What if they found out?"

"Chances are, they wouldn't. There is a risk, though. You'd have to be aware of that. But you can be sure we'd have some men nearby."

"Look," she said, "I didn't ask for any of this. I wasn't even the one who got my family involved. All I want is to live my life and raise my child—"

She turned away and tried to control herself. She could imagine how it sounded. As though she were blaming the police for the whole thing.

"I don't know if I could do it," she sobbed. "I'd just be getting myself into worse trouble."

"What will you do, then?" he asked.

"I don't know. Maybe I'll go away somewhere. I don't know where, but that's what my husband did. Maybe it's the only thing to do."

"It's up to you ma'am."

"I'll think about it. What you said."

"I'd suggest you come into the station tomorrow morning and talk it over, before you make any decision. What I told you is just a general procedure. You could find out how they'd want to handle this case, and what the risks might be."

"Thanks," said Pauline. "But I have to tell you, I feel let down. I know all those stupid rules are set up to protect the rights of criminals. What about *my* rights?"

"It's not a perfect system," he admitted.

"It stinks."

She watched him go out to his car, and locked both doors after him.

Damn you, Jarvis. Damn you, damn you.

She walked around the living room, mentally adding up the value of its contents.

The antique Chinese chest and the nesting tables. Possibly one or two thousand. The silver vase and the Imari plate. A few hundred? Most of the other furnishings were merely old, not antiques, and some were new. She would not get much for any of those. It wasn't easy to sell secondhand furniture. Dealers wanted whole estates, not a few pieces.

In the den, the large color television with remote control. The antique desk. The file cabinet. You couldn't give away a file cabinet.

The dining room set was old but probably not antique. The highboy was antique. A thousand? Then there was the outdoor barbeque on the patio in back. Maybe fifty dollars for that. She had forgotten the painting over the fireplace—not worth much, because the artist was unknown—and the stereo in the living room.

Upstairs, another, smaller television set. Another, smaller stereo. The beds were mostly new, the dressers old. Who would she sell it all to? And would it come to forty thousand? Scratch that—forty-six thousand.

Nowhere near it, even with all her clothes thrown in.

She had no furs and very little jewelry that might be sale-able.

The house and even her car were in his name. She would have to have him declared dead. She would have to wait seven years for that, and by then, she and Kirby would be long dead themselves.

Oh, God, Kirby. She had read about children falling down old wells. It took days for either rescue or death.

She had to stop this. It was getting her nowhere.

No matter which way she turned, it all came back to one thing. She needed her parents. It was inconceivable that she couldn't reach them. In desperation she looked through the wastebasket for the number of the Florida campground.

She dialed and listened. They had to be there. It was life or death.

The telephone rang on and on. Because it was night-time and no one was in the campground office. And her parents were not there anyway. They had gone on, per-haps farther north, now that it was summer.

Her friend Suzanne. Sue Rhinehart. Sue and Les would help her. They were among the few people, maybe the only people in all of Allenbury, who knew just how far the Kingsleys had fallen. She could talk to them.

She waited again while the telephone rang. It was late, but they wouldn't turn off the phone. People always kept it open in case of emergency.

But no one answered, and she remembered that they had gone away. A family trip to Mystic. They planned to stay until Tuesday. And that meant Tuesday night. She couldn't wait that long.

"I don't believe it," she muttered to herself. "I don't

34

believe it."

Who else? There were only a few close friends. Really close. The kind she could turn to for a thing like this.

Maybe Jane Brighton. She was not quite like Sue, but she was in town. They were not taking their vacation until August.

Again she listened to the ringing. She felt a wild elation when it broke and Jane answered.

"I'm sorry if I woke you," Pauline began. "It's an emergency. I'm in terrible trouble, Jane."

She related all that had happened that evening. Jane laughed at first, not believing her story. Then she asked why the police couldn't help.

"Because," said Pauline, "the men haven't done anything yet. We have to wait until Kirby gets hit by a car."

"Are you going to take that seriously?"

"Of course I'm going to take it seriously! I've read about things like that, haven't you?"

"I wish I could help."

Jane didn't want to get involved.

"So do I," Pauline said, "but I'll manage. And right now, I haven't time to talk."

She went to the den and looked in Jarvis's desk for their bankbook. As she had thought, there was very little in it. Eleven dollars, just enough to hold the account. Hardly worth the time it would take her to close it. She would have to manage on the hundred Jarvis had left her, and whatever was in her purse. But where would she go?

They would all be like Jane. Afraid. Who wouldn't be afraid of people like that? Or perhaps not willing to be bothered.

With only a hundred dollars to her name, the first thing she needed was a job. At the time of her marriage, until Kirby arrived, she had worked at *Fifth Avenue* magazine.

And Dudley Morgan, her good friend, was still there. He was rather important at *Fifth Avenue* now. Important enough to put in a word for her.

He wouldn't mind the late hour. Dudley never minded. The phone was answered on the second ring.

"This is Dudley Morgan. Thanks for calling. I'm sorry I can't talk with you right now. When you hear the beep, please leave your name and number..."

The beep took her by surprise. She had been trying to think what she could tell him.

"It's Pauline Kingsley, in Connecticut. Listen, Dudley, I'm coming to the city with my little girl, no husband, and I need a job. Can you help? Please call just as soon as you can, *please*. And thank you."

She hung up, wondering whether he had turned on the machine because he was out or because he was sleeping. She and Jarvis did it sometimes when they didn't want to be disturbed.

She had forgotten about the answering machine in her preparations for leaving. It would be one way she could stay in touch without actually revealing where she was. She looked for the remote key, so she could phone in and get the messages off the machine, but couldn't find it. Jarvis must have taken it with him.

She settled down to wait, expecting, hoping that at any moment the phone would ring. She had very little time.

5

It was still dark when Jarvis Kingsley woke from a half sleep in the front seat of his car. Since leaving home, he had driven for almost twenty-four hours and rested for six.

He had stayed mostly on secondary roads and traveled in devious circles. In spite of the miles he had covered and the time he had spent, he was still only in Pennsylvania. He had headed west because it was almost all there was. From Connecticut, it was not possible to go very far east, but he wondered if perhaps west was too predictable.

Although daybreak was a long way off, the sky was beginning to lighten. He looked around to get his bearings. It had been too dark to see very much when he pulled off the main road.

The darkness notwithstanding, he seemed to have made a good choice. He was parked under a grove of trees next to a cow pasture. Its stubbly grass was soaked with dew and the air was hazy with a rising mist. He had heard rain last night during his uneasy sleep. Now it was evaporating. The mist was everywhere, in his car and all through his clothes.

He looked back warily, hearing the hiss of tires on wet pavement. In the distance, he saw a flash of headlights. He hadn't realized that he was so close to the highway.

He ached from fatigue and his cramped sleeping position, but knew he would have to get moving again. Almost certainly they had a description of his car. Maybe even the license number. He could be overreacting, but it wasn't worth the chance.

He eased his car out onto a narrow lane, then headed back to the highway. Even at that hour, people seemed to be on the road in large numbers. He took the precaution of checking every car that drew near him.

He couldn't go on like this. He needed a different car, a safe place to stay. Ever since last week when he had shown up without his payment, stupidly hoping to plead for more time, he had seen himself beaten and bloodied, or washed up on a beach, shackled and weighted with cement blocks. Sometimes they literally extracted their pound of flesh, chunk by chunk until the victim bled to death. He had heard that, too.

He couldn't sell the house. He had already taken out a mortgage on it, and his share of the proceeds would not cover his debt. He would lose it anyway now, because he couldn't meet the mortgage payments, but at least it would remain standing. If he signed it over to the Broker, they would burn it to the ground and collect the insurance.

Even more than the house, they had wanted his business. His Venus Press. They liked the fact that he was publishing erotica. They would take his outlets, his contacts and mailing lists, and would sell hard-core pornography under the imprint of Venus Press. It was his publishing house, associated with his name. They would ruin him forever, perhaps even get him imprisoned.

He would give them their damned money someday, but not all the so-called interest. That was an outrage.

He didn't know how far their power extended, but they could follow him anywhere if they wanted to. They couldn't let him live. It would set an undesirable precedent. He wished he could have explained to Pauline what had happened. She would take it personally, his disappearing like this, but at least her innocence would keep her safe.

Even more than that, he didn't know how he could explain to anyone, least of all Pauline, what he had done. Five percent a week. He remembered thinking what a bargain it was. And he, Jarvis Kingsley, had always considered himself intelligent.

In his rear-view mirror he could see a pink glow in the east. It would be coming up soon. He would have to decide what to do.

Maybe he could head for the south. They wouldn't expect that. What would they expect? Canada, maybe. He would go to Atlanta, which he had heard was a boom town, change his name and get some kind of factory job.

What about Social Security? Anybody could call himself something else, but a guy needed documents. That got into a whole new ball game of forged papers. His life heretofore had all been on the level. He had no idea how to go about getting a false ID, one that would stand up to scrutiny. There were channels, he supposed, but you had to be a certain kind of person and have led a certain kind of life even to know what those channels were.

That black car in back of him. It had been there for several miles. His hands tightened on the wheel. Never before had he felt this physical fear. He had been feeling it since that day last week, the day his payment was due.

He increased his speed. The car kept pace with him. He dropped back and drifted right to let it pass. When it did, he saw a lone woman driver. His muscles relaxed and he drew a welcome breath.

By the time he reached the next town, near the Ohio border, the sun was up. In Ohio he would stop for breakfast and try to develop an overall plan. Maybe he would sell the car. Maybe buy a new one, or better yet, take a bus somewhere. He hadn't firmly decided on the south. There was always California and his sister, Anne. She would take care of him. He hated to get back into that old role, but it was comforting to know she was there.

On second thought, they might be able to trace him to Anne's. Besides, he didn't want to drag her into this.

It made him think again, queasily, of Pauline. But that was a different situation. Pauline was not an accessory after the fact, as Anne would be. Pauline knew nothing about it. Aside from his shame, he had kept her ignorant for her own protection. What could they do to her, when she didn't know anything about it?

He found a diner on the edge of some village, near a single line of railroad track. It was already open for breakfast, and a truck was parked in front of it. He set his own car at an angle so the license plate would not be visible from the road, and went inside.

Surreptitiously he checked out the truck driver, who

was sitting at one end of the counter. It made him realize how paranoid he was getting. He took a stool near the middle, and the redheaded waitress handed him a menu.

He debated whether to save his money, or try to gain some strength to face the day. He decided on strength, and ordered pancakes, sausages, and two fried eggs. It was cheap enough, out here in the boondocks.

While his sausages were frying, the waitress looked him over. "You a salesman?" she asked.

"That's right." He grinned at the new identity that had just been handed to him.

"Yeah? What do you sell? Anything interesting?" Her manner was casually flirtatious. It was a role she played. She probably had a husband, whom she would call her "old man," and six kids.

"Uh—" Books were too close, but Venus was still on his mind. "Ladies' underwear. Lingerie. High-class stuff."

She giggled. He wished he had thought before he spoke. She might want to see his samples.

"I sell directly to the stores," he explained. "It's just like any other kind of merchandise. I don't get to do the actual fitting."

Both the waitress and the truck driver laughed, and Jarvis laughed with them. He wasn't doing too badly. If it were not for that stumbling block of documents, he could assume a new personality quite easily.

"Where are you headed?" the waitress asked as she served him his breakfast.

"All over. I'm the midwest rep. This is my first trip." In case the questions called for more detail, he turned his attention to the sausages.

41

"Where are you from?"

"Indiana." It popped into his head, a midwest state. He hoped she would not ask where in Indiana.

"You're not much for talking, are you?"

Not when the questions might get hairy. "I've got a sort of headache," he explained with a wan smile. "All those fumes on the road."

"You want an aspirin? I've got aspirin. On the house."

"No, it's okay. I just took something."

The truck driver slapped a bill onto the counter and left. A family came in, father, mother, son and daughter. They kept things busy enough so that Jarvis was left alone.

The food and the coffee made him feel better. He still hadn't decided what to do, but he would think of something. He gave himself a deadline for making up his mind. Eleven A.M.

He left a generous tip and went out to his car. He should have had all this planned, but it hadn't even occurred to him. He had thought he could reason with them. Get an extension of time. He hadn't realized there was no such thing.

California, he thought again. They would never go that far, even if they figured he was there.

But they were adamant. If they didn't follow him to California to get their money back, what would they do?

"Oh, my God," he whispered as the answer crashed down on him. "Oh, my God."

6

She tried to sleep, but couldn't. The whole thing seemed unreal, unthinkable, yet she knew it had happened. Now everything depended upon hearing from Dudley.

Please, just call.

Dudley was too polite to call in the middle of the night.

After waiting for all eternity, she watched the sun come up. It was not quite six. In another hour, he would be getting up to go to work.

At seven-thirty, she tried calling again. And once again, the machine answered.

"Dudley, it's me, Pauline," she said to it. "Please call me *now*. I have to leave here soon. Please, *now*."

She couldn't wait. There must be someone else. Dudley could help her find a job, but she needed shelter, too.

There was Pam Bates. She and Pam had worked together and enjoyed complaining together about their lowly jobs at *Fifth Avenue*. They had gotten married at about the same time, and now Pam lived in Forest Hills. She looked up the number. A moment later she was listening to the telephone ring. And ring. Somewhere in Forest Hills.

So early? How could they have gone anywhere this early? Damn summer. They were probably away on vacation. Or else their offices opened at eight.

She paged through her address book. It was filled with numbers for babysitters and Chinese restaurants. And friends who had moved to California. If she set out driving—but they could easily follow her car.

There was another *Fifth Avenue* person. Karyn Hargitty, in Greenwich Village.

She hesitated. Karyn was not a close friend, but more an acquaintance. Would she help? It was a terrible thing to ask of anybody. A horrible thing to have to admit to anyone.

After a few rings, a muffled voice answered the phone.

"Karyn?" Pauline asked. "Karyn Hargitty? This is Pauline Kingsley, you know, from the magazine. Is this Karyn? You don't sound like you. Did I wake you?"

"You did," Karyn replied. And then, "Pauline?"

"I'm really sorry I woke you. I thought it would be late enough."

"I'm calling in sick today." Karyn sounded fretful. "I have a cold."

"Oh, I'm sorry. I'm really sorry. But, Karyn, I've got a terrible problem. I'm about to go into the city with my little girl. I have to leave home because we were threatened. My husband got mixed up with these people— loan sharks—and they threatened to hurt my child. I have to get out of here."

44

"Pauline, is this a joke?"

"No, it isn't. You're the second person who thought that. I couldn't dream up a thing like this. I need a place to stay for a couple of days. It wouldn't be long."

"I'd like to help you," Karyn said, "but I only have a one-room apartment, and I've got this cold, and uh—my niece is here with me for the summer."

"I understand," said Pauline. "Thanks, Karyn. Go back to sleep."

"Call me sometime."

"I will."

She wouldn't. And it was a lie about the niece, she was sure.

She called Dudley's number again. At the sound of the machine's bright message, she slammed down the receiver.

A few minutes later, Kirby came into the room and asked why she was packing.

"Because we're going somewhere," Pauline replied. "We're going for a long ride, just you and me. We'll have fun together."

"Where are we going?"

"To a big city."

She stopped and tried to recall her telephone conversations. She didn't think she had named the city, but she had mentioned the word several times, and it wouldn't be hard to guess which one. Nobody would think she meant Bridgeport.

Stupid. Even in her own home, she should not have said anything about her destination. Who could tell what that idiot might have been doing last night when he roamed the house? He could have planted a bug. Maybe they had bugged the phone. She was sure they would have anticipated her flight. They had even warned her against it, but what choice did she have? They would figure that out, too.

Kirby tagged after her, trying to understand what was happening. "Mommy, are we sleeping over?"

"Of course we're sleeping over. Here, let me pack your blanket. You don't want to leave that behind." The trauma of being uprooted was hard enough. This was no time to separate Kirby from her blanket.

"I want to wait for Daddy."

Florida. If only she could get to Florida, whether or not she found her parents.

But they might be followed. They would have to go the wrong way. She couldn't even take her car. And without money, she could never get that far.

"Can we see Grandma?" Kirby asked.

"I wish we could. Maybe later."

What if her parents tried to reach her, as undoubtedly they would? She couldn't have them worrying. They would come looking for her and they wouldn't find her. Instead the two men might find them.

She went downstairs to the telephone answering machine in the den and recorded a new announcement.

"This is Pauline. I'm sorry you can't reach us right now. As soon as I can, I'll try to get a message to you through your last address. You know the one I mean. I'll explain then."

She put their letter in her purse and finished packing. She had only a small suitcase and a nylon shoulder bag. It was all the luggage she dared carry. They must be unencumbered and inconspicuous.

She unplugged the clocks and the instant-on television sets. There was no sense in running up an electric bill. The refrigerator should have been turned off, too, but she had no time to clean it. She scrawled a note to the post office to hold the mail, and another to the newspaper boy to stop delivery.

She locked the house, every window and every outside door. This was her home, yet somehow it already seemed remote. It was past.

Her first stop was the neighbors' house. Inez Collins answered the door in her nightgown and hair rollers, with a tall, tinkling glass in her hand.

"Hel-*lo*, there. Going somewhere?"

"I have to," Pauline said. "Jarvis was in an accident. I've got to go to him. I was wondering if you could watch the house for me."

"Where will you be?"

"Thanks so much. I really appreciate—"

"Is it bad? Where is he?"

"Quite bad. I have to run."

"When will you be back?"

"Thanks so much, Inez. I really appreciate it." Pauline got back into the car. She had managed to deflect that barrage of questions. It would be her last encounter in Allenbury.

She drove along Dogwood Road, past solid, affluent homes and spacious lawns. She had belonged there, once. No longer. She was a refugee. A refugee from Dogwood Road.

As they entered the village, she watched for a long, black car. There were many such cars, Cadillacs and Continentals, gliding down the tree-lined main street or parked in front of the carefully coordinated half-timbered storefronts. Solid, affluent Allenbury, where there were no slums. She was a refugee from Allenbury.

She drove five miles to North Port, which did have slums, and left the car in an A & P parking lot near the railroad station. She bought a ticket for New Haven and led Kirby across an overpass to the northbound platform.

The train was late. She had been afraid of that. It left her exposed and vulnerable for fifteen minutes. But she could see the whole parking area. She could see everyone who came in. And they would expect her to be on the southbound side.

Finally, in the distance the train appeared, curling around a bend. She watched for last-minute arrivals as she stood poised to board. Then they were on the train and it was pulling out of the station. They were safe.

The ride to New Haven took less than half an hour. When they reached it, she checked once more to be sure they had not been followed, and bought a ticket for New York. As they left the ticket window, Kirby complained that she was hungry.

"Couldn't you wait until we get there?" Pauline asked. She was immediately sorry. It would be hours before they got anywhere, and a four-year-old's hunger couldn't wait.

"All right, I'll buy you a sandwich. But you'll have to eat fast so we can catch the next train." She found a luncheonette and ordered an egg salad sandwich for Kirby.

As always, Kirby ate slowly. Pauline fidgeted and urged her along, trying to be gentle about it. Trying not to look at her watch every few seconds.

48

She thought of calling Dudley from there. But he would be at work. And he would still be at work when she reached the city, and then it would be a local call. She would not let herself think that he might be on vacation. They couldn't all be away. Not the Rhineharts, and Pam Bates, and Dudley, too.

As they hurried to catch the train, Kirby asked, "Why do we have to keep going somewhere?"

"We're going to a new home," Pauline said. "A brand new home."

"I want my house with you and Daddy."

"We'll go back there soon, but not today." And maybe not so soon, and not with Daddy. They boarded the train as its doors were closing. She guided Kirby to the end of the car where two empty seats faced each other.

Kirby looked out of the window. "Why can't we find Daddy?"

"Honey, I don't know where he is right now."

What if Jarvis tried to get in touch with them?

Tough, Pauline thought as she lifted her bags to the rack above the seat. How would he like to get in touch with her and find that his daughter had fallen down an old well?

Between the traveling and the anxiety, Kirby was already tired. Pauline settled her on a seat by herself, so that she could lie down.

"I don't want to sleep," Kirby protested.

"You'd better. We still have a lot of today ahead of us."

"But you might go away."

"No, I won't, honey. I promise I'll stay right here."

Pauline rested her own head against the window and closed her eyes. She hadn't slept at all last night. The motion of the train lulled her, but the next instant she was jolted awake by her thoughts.

It really happened. Those two men.

She wondered where Jarvis was now, and what had been going through his mind when he left her to face it alone. He probably hadn't imagined that they would come to her. Maybe he even thought that, by leaving, he was keeping her out of it.

Oh, Jarvis. Hopelessly impractical, she had called him. But couldn't he at least try?

She remembered the years in college, where they had met. College was Jarvis's milieu. He should have stayed there, become a professor in an ivory tower. She remembered the afternoons when they used to get together and read Chaucer or Shakespeare. Somehow, probably from a book, he had learned to speak both Chaucerian and Elizabethan English. They had discovered new vistas, reading the poets as they had meant their words to be spoken. Othello: "I took by the throat the circumcised dog and smote him thus." Pronounced with hard C's instead of soft, the line became a death rattle.

Kirby. She shouldn't have thought of death.

Oh, Jarvis. We used to be so happy.

She found a tissue in her purse and wiped her eyes, stifling a sob so as not to disturb Kirby. A woman across the aisle watched her curiously and Pauline froze, managing to stifle everything.

7

She gazed out of the train window, thinking of their imminent arrival in the city and what her next step would be.

And Jarvis.

Had they been such strangers after all? Or had he gone a little crazy, a kind of psychosis from being out of work? It was not only the money, it was the self-esteem.

Kirby opened her eyes and sat up. "Mommy, how much more?"

"Just a little bit. Do you see all those buildings out there? It means we're in the city now."

"Then why aren't we there?"

"Because it's a big place. This is only one part of the city. We're going to another part."

Kirby looked dazed. "I don't want the city."

"Oh, you'll like it. It's pretty at night, with all the lights, and there are so many things to do."

The train rattled into the underground approach to Grand Central Terminal. Kirby was fascinated by the black tunnel dotted with pinpoints of signal lights, but when the train stopped and they got off, she walked with her head down. It was already mid-afternoon.

"Are you tired?" Pauline asked.

Kirby began to cry. "I don't like it here."

They were still on the platform in the tunnel, walking endlessly toward a ramp that would lead them into the station.

"This isn't where we're going to be staying," Pauline assured her. "Nobody likes this part of it. Will a chocolate bar make you feel better?" Kirby sniffled. When they reached the concourse, Pauline found a newsstand and bought a Hershey bar with almonds.

"And now for a telephone."

In a corridor just off the main concourse there were banks of telephones, and directories for every major city. Parking Kirby and the luggage where she could see them, Pauline closed herself into a booth.

A crisp voice answered, *"Fifth Avenue* magazine, may I help you?"

"Dudley Morgan, please."

"Mr. Morgan isn't here any more," said the operator. "He left about three weeks ago."

"Well—do you know where he went? Where is he working now?"

"I don't know that. I'm sorry."

"Wait. Does anybody there know—"

"I don't think so. I think he was taking some time off. Miss, I have to answer another call."

Damn, she thought as she hung up. Of all the times for Dudley to quit. He had been there for years.

She dialed his home number. She was elated when the

phone rang a third time. That was a change from the answering machine. She would hear his voice instead of a recorded message.

The phone continued to ring. He had to be there. If he had turned off the machine, it meant he had come back since her last call.

Or come back and gone out again, and forgotten to turn the machine back on.

Even if he had gotten her message, he wouldn't be able to reach her now. She would have to keep trying. The night was only a few hours away and they needed a place to sleep. If they couldn't find that, she needed some prospect of a job so that she would dare spend the last of her money on a cheap hotel.

She could go down and camp on his doorstep. But he might not come at all. He might have guests. He might be in the middle of an affair.

She remembered his apartment. It was in a row of small brick buildings on East Twenty-ninth Street. She had it in her address book.

East Twenty-ninth Street. East Twenties. It made her think of Ernie Hampden.

Ernie had been married to Jarvis's sister, Anne. He was, as Pauline remembered, a very kind but unexciting person. Not long after the senior Kingsleys were killed in an accident, about the time Kirby was born, Anne had divorced him. Out of boredom, it seemed. Ernie was too much of a good guy for her.

Anne must have felt some guilt about it, especially when she next took up with a man barely out of his teens. She left Ernie a large portion of her inheritance, which he used to open a restaurant somewhere in the

East Twenties.

Pauline had no record of Ernie's address or phone number. Their ways had parted after the divorce. She went out to look in the directory, and was grabbed around the leg by Kirby.

"Please don't leave the luggage, honey. It's all we have and somebody might take it."

Drooping with fatigue and despair, Kirby returned to her place on top of the suitcase. Pauline relented, and went to give her a hug.

"I'm sorry, baby. I know this is hard, but we'll be out of here soon. Even if we have to sleep in Ernie's restaurant."

She could not remember the name of the place. She knew it included Ernie's name somewhere, but couldn't recall whether it was his first or last name. She flipped through the pages of the directory, looking for Hampden, Ernest.

No such person was listed.

Oh, hell, she thought. *He's gone.*

She turned to the Yellow Pages. It seemed as though a major portion of the two-inch-thick book was devoted to restaurants. She began systematically. Hampden. There was no restaurant that had a name starting with Hampden.

All right, then, Ernest.

And no restaurant whose name started with Ernest. But Ernie? Yes, there was an Ernie's!

Anybody could be named Ernie. She didn't dare hope. She opened her change purse and counted out several dimes.

"I think we might be getting somewhere," she told

Kirby, and went back to the booths. She dialed Ernie's. Someone with a heavy accent informed her that the owner was not Ernie Hampden. She pronounced the name several times to be sure, and so did he. He had never heard of Ernie Hampden.

Ernies Bar & Grill did not know a Hampden, either.

Ernesto's. Would he be so flamboyant? Something loomed beside her, giving her a start. It was a man waiting to use the phone book.

"Oh, I'm sorry." She scribbled down the number for Ernesto's and went into a booth. As she had suspected, it was another wasted dime.

The man was still paging through the book. All the other directories were in use. She put in the time trying to call Dudley again, and then Pam Bates in Forest Hills. There was no answer at either place. She could not remember whether Pam still had a job, or if she did, where it was.

At any rate, Pam had a husband, and safety, and a comfortable home in Forest Hills, while Pauline didn't even have a place to spend the night. There were benches in Grand Central's waiting room, but the station closed down during the early hours of the morning.

What would they do? Would the Salvation Army take them in? She didn't know New York anymore. Since Kirby's birth, she had made very few trips to the city.

Kirby rose from the suitcase and came toward her, dragging her feet. Pauline ran to intercept her.

"Please, baby, I asked you to stay with the luggage. We don't want to lose it."

She led Kirby back to the bags. "I'll buy you another candy bar in a minute." But at that moment the directory became free.

She found the page where she had left off and began running her eyes down the columns, searching for addresses, for a name that might be familiar. It took her a minute or two to discover an additional listing of restaurants by ethnic type. She checked under "American."

There was nothing with either Ernest or Hampden in it. As far as she knew, his cuisine was plain American, but not all the restaurants were included in that listing.

"You gonna be there all night, lady?"

Again she had to give up the book. She bought Kirby her promised chocolate bar and then went back to scanning the columns, page by page.

She had had no contact with Ernie in several years. For all she knew, he might have given up the restaurant and left the city. This was only a chance, like all the others. She would try Dudley again in a little while.

Suddenly she stopped and went back. She could scarcely believe it. Uncle Ernie's Steak House. She reached for her pen to write it down.

At that moment, something made her look up. Some primitive instinct for self-preservation.

Over there, in the corridor where the train gates were. She couldn't be sure, but it reminded her of the fat man. He was facing the other way. Watching for someone.

Could it be? She seized Kirby with one hand and the baggage with the other. In a city of eight million people, how could it be? They must have followed her, or known where she was going. It probably wasn't the fat man at all, but she couldn't take a chance.

She darted through a passage way that led to the waiting room. And the women's rest room. It was the only

56

safe place she could think of. When she was sure they were hidden, she set down the bags and tried to catch her breath.

Kirby looked up at her, subdued and frightened. "Mommy? Why did you run like that?"

"There was somebody there," Pauline explained, "and I didn't want him to see us. I know you don't understand, but you might as well know. If anybody tries to talk to you or make friends with you, run and find me, okay? And especially if they want you to go with them. Can you remember that?"

"How long do we have to stay here?"

"I don't know, baby. I just don't know."

Kirby sat on the suitcase while Pauline rested against the wall. Women came in and went out and stared at them. Kirby cried that she didn't want to stay there anymore.

"Just a little longer," Pauline said. "And things are going to get better very soon. They can't get too much worse."

"I want to go home."

"Please stop saying that. I want to go home, too, but we can't, right now."

"Why can't we?"

"Because something happened at home. We can't go back there for a while. We have to stay here where it's safe."

Kirby wept with a low, humming wail. Tears rolled down her cheeks. Pauline felt wrenched, certain that it was all for nothing. It couldn't possibly have been the man. But what if it was?

"Honey, please don't cry. Some old lady is going to

come over here and tell me I'm abusing you, and that's all we need. We have to stay invisible. Pretend you're part of the wall."

She tried to make a game out of invisibility. Kirby was intrigued for a while and then began to cry again.

"I don't want to stay in here. I want to go home."

"Maybe when we get enough money, we'll go—"

To live with her parents, at least for a while. As soon as she had a place to sit down and a sheet of paper, she would write to them at the Florida campground. She would mark it "Hold for Arrival."

But what if they never got her message? They only phoned about once a month when there was something important to say. If they didn't phone, she would never find them. She did not dare give a forwarding address to the Allenbury post office.

"Do you want to use the john?" she asked. "We might as well take advantage of being in here." But even that occupied them for no more than five minutes.

It was six o'clock in the evening. They had been in the rest room for an hour, losing valuable time.

She rummaged in her suitcase and found a pink paisley rain scarf. She tied it around her head and put on a pair of sunglasses.

"Don't I look different now?" she asked brightly. "Just call me Superman, the quick change artist."

She opened the rest room door and looked carefully in both directions.

"It's crazy, isn't it?" she said to Kirby. "I used to have nightmares about being chased, but this is the first time it's really happened."

They went back to the telephones. She kept Kirby

with her while she looked up the number again for Uncle Ernie's Steak House and wrote it in her address book. *Thank God.*

She left the door of the booth open, with the baggage at her feet and Kirby leaning against her knee. First she tried Dudley's number again. She let it ring twenty times. Then Pamela Bates. Then she dialed the number for the restaurant and waited, listening to the long and regular buzz of the ringer.

No, she thought, *you've got to be there.*

Somebody had to be there. It was six o'clock in the evening. If they were not open for dinner, when were they open? She broke the connection and tried again. She went outside and checked the number in the directory. Then she dialed it again, watching carefully to see that she did it right.

Finally she hung up and sat dejectedly.

"He's got to be in the phone book," she said, and tried again to find a home listing for Ernie. She tried the directories for all five boroughs. There was always a chance that he might have sold the place, but why would they have kept his name? Or he might have closed for two weeks and gone to vacation in the Bahamas.

"I know what we'll do. We'll take a bus and go down there. Maybe they're just too busy to answer the phone."

Carrying the bags, and with Kirby dragging wearily, they went out to Lexington Avenue and waited for a downtown bus. The rush-hour crowds had thinned, but still the bus was full and they had to stand. Kirby clung to her, and a fat woman complained that Pauline's suitcase was in the way of her feet.

"You should be glad that's all you have to worry

about," Pauline told her coldly. She tried to keep her balance and hold Kirby from falling as they jerked and rocked down Lexington Avenue. By crouching, she could see out of the window to follow the street numbers, since she did not really know where the restaurant was. When the numbers seemed about right, she pushed her way down the packed aisle to reach the door. Kirby clutched fearfully at her arm.

"It's all right, honey, we won't lose each other," Pauline assured her. "Now there's just a little more walking. It should be on this side of the street."

After half a block, she saw the awning. She began to walk faster.

And there it was, not glossy, but traditional and nondescript. Unimaginative, comfortably mellow, like Ernie himself. A long green and white checked cafe curtain ran the length of the plate glass window. The name of the restaurant was lettered in gold above it. Inside she could see the tables set with water glasses turned upside-down to keep out the dust. On the door was a large hand-lettered sign: CLOSED MONDAYS.

She stood under a tree, shaded by the buildings from the evening sun, and felt heat rise from the sidewalk. She had forgotten how hot the city could be in summer.

"Our bad luck is holding, baby. It's closed."

She looked around for someone, anyone, who might be able to help. Two doors away was a small delicatessen. She went inside and asked the man behind the counter, "Do you know Ernie Hampden of Ernie's Steak House?"

"Nope," said the man as he gazed beyond her shoulder.

60

"Do you know anybody who would know him? Or know where I could find him?"

"Lady, I already told you I don't know the guy."

Kirby tugged at her hand. "Mommy, I'm hungry."

"We're not getting anything here," said Pauline as they left the store.

She checked the nearby apartment houses, looking for his name on a doorbell. "Well . . . can you stand a little more walking? We're going over to Dudley's place."

Kirby trudged beside her, too tired to protest.

Dudley's apartment was farther east than she remembered. The walk stretched on, seemingly for block after block in the evening heat. And then came a rush of familiarity as she descended three steps, pushed open a heavy glass door, and found his name in the middle of a row of mailboxes with a doorbell under each one.

D. Morgan. The box above it was crammed with mail.

"Oh, Kirby, honey."

"What?" Kirby asked.

"He's not here. I don't believe it. I can't believe there's nobody to help us."

She should not have said that. She mustn't let Kirby know how desperate their situation was.

"I guess it's back to Grand Central." She tried to sound cheerful about it. "I only wish they didn't close at night." Briefly she considered the Port Authority Bus Terminal. But it was a dismal, horrible place. She wouldn't spend a day there, much less a night.

"I only wish Daddy could see us now," she said as they walked back to Third Avenue and took a bus uptown.

Kirby groaned when they reentered Grand Central.

"I know you're as sick of this place as I am," Pauline

said, "but right now I don't know where else to go. This will have to be our base of operations for a while."

"We could go home," Kirby said hopefully.

"Not yet, sweetheart. When you're older and can understand, I'll explain it to you."

She bought hot dogs for their dinner, a bag of potato chips for Kirby, and a newspaper for herself. While they ate, she studied the want ads. Even if she found a job right away, it would be at least a week or two before she received any pay. How would they live until then?

She would not wait for Dudley. She would try her old office before anything else. *Fifth Avenue* magazine described itself as a "sophisticated experience in smart living, arts, and travel." She hardly looked the part now. She felt it even less.

Besides, it had been five years since she worked there. They wouldn't remember her. She had not amounted to much even then. In taking the job, she hadn't realized that Editorial Assistant was a glorified name for go-fer. It was a position that, in the want ads for more down-to-earth business concerns, was identified as "Gal Friday."

Furthermore, being a glamorous periodical, *Fifth Avenue* could find all it needed of bright young women fresh out of college. She hadn't even that to offer anymore. She had nothing. She could barely type with two fingers, much less use a word processor, or whatever they were doing these days.

"Mommy, can I say it please?"

"Say what, honey?"

"When—are—we—going—home?"

Pauline stopped to consider. Her brain, starved and exhausted, worked slowly. "No, you may not say it." She

62

folded the newspaper. She simply couldn't think anymore.

"It did say closed Mondays, didn't it? So it should be open on Tuesdays. Maybe we ought to try camping out there. Sleeping in the doorway like shopping bag women."

Kirby looked at her with glazed eyes. They wouldn't really, of course, go back downtown. Pauline was beginning to formulate a plan for how they would spend the night.

They settled on a bench in the waiting room. She wrapped Kirby in her pink blanket, making her as comfortable as possible, but did not lie down herself for fear they would be thrown out as loiterers.

Now and then she dozed, still sitting up, but for the most part, tried to stay alert and watchful. She thought of home and her comfortable bed. Only last night—but she hadn't slept last night, either.

And Kirby blamed her for all the discomfort and inconvenience. It didn't seem fair, but maybe it was her fault that they had done this stupid thing. Maybe she would have been better off cooperating with the police. She had been too frightened to think rationally.

But it would have taken time to get the trap set, and she didn't think the men intended to give her much time. And even if she managed to pull it off, what about afterward, when the men were out on bail? And after the trial, when they had been acquitted by their high-powered lawyers and a cowed or gullible jury?

Gradually the waiting room emptied. They were almost the only people remaining. A man in a ragged suit walked past her. A homeless habitué, she assumed.

"Mister," she called to him, "does this place really close at night?"

He gave her a bleary stare. "Yes, ma'am," he said, and walked on.

Gently she roused her child. "Kirby, honey, we have to leave here now. We'll walk a few blocks to a very pretty place. You'll like it. It's near the river."

"Don't wanna walk anymore," Kirby mumbled.

"Well, I can't carry you, because I have the bags. You come with me and then you can sleep again for the whole rest of the night."

Kirby wept softly as they went out through the Park Avenue exit. Pauline would have been willing to spend money on a bus, but no buses were in sight. They turned east and started up Forty-second Street. Kirby stumbled beside her, clinging to her hand. The suitcases weighed down her other arm.

"Isn't it warm here!" Pauline exclaimed. "It doesn't cool off much even at night, as I remember. That's because all the stone and concrete hold the heat. I think that's the reason."

She did not expect a reply and didn't get one. The few blocks were longer than she had recollected, and most of the way was uphill. Finally they reached First Avenue. Across the street, the glass slab of the United Nations building rose dimly gleaming into the night sky. Beyond it was the East River, reflecting the lights of Queens.

"Here we are," she said. They were in a tiny park at the foot of a concrete wall. It was little more than a few fenced-in areas of ivy surrounded by benches and trees and lit at intervals by street lamps.

Except for the First Avenue truck traffic, it was quiet

64

and peaceful in the night. And probably fairly safe, she thought. The United Nations security police were not far away.

On one of the benches at the other end of the park, a drunk slept on a bed of newspapers. If he could stay there without being chased away, perhaps they could too. She found a place in the shadow of a tree.

"I never thought I'd come to this," she said as Kirby snuggled beside her.

8

She waited for daybreak across the East River. It was the longest night she had ever spent. She felt tired to the point of lightheadedness. At any moment she would probably start to hallucinate.

Kirby stirred. It was light now, but still too early to do anything.

"We'll go back to the station, and wash up and get something to eat," Pauline said when Kirby was fully awake. "Then we'll go down to Ernie's and hope he's open for lunch."

Kirby looked about, baffled, and disheveled from her sleep. "Why are we outdoors?"

"Good question. But don't you think it's a pretty place?"

"No."

They began the walk back to Grand Central. It was early yet for rush-hour traffic. The streets were peaceful, the day moist and fresh. A new beginning. Today they would have to find someone who could help them.

They entered the station at Lexington Avenue. Already people were beginning to come off the trains. She had never known that anyone commuted so early.

"Are we here again?" Kirby asked in dismay when they reached the telephone area.

"I just want to call a couple of friends. If they're in town at all, I should be able to get them now."

She tried Pam Bates first, letting the phone ring twenty times. Two full minutes. Next she called Dudley and again rang for two minutes.

"Well," she said to Kirby, "I guess that wipes out plans one and two. Shall we go and wash up?"

At the door to the rest room, Kirby turned rigid. "I don't like it in there."

"I don't blame you," Pauline said, "but don't you want to use the toilet? We won't stay this time."

They rinsed their faces and Pauline applied fresh make-up. Nothing could hide the grayish tinge or the shadows of exhaustion.

After a breakfast of doughnuts and orange juice, she called the restaurant. Kirby watched her hopefully. There was no answer.

"We'll try again in a little while," Pauline said as they returned to the waiting room, where she bought a *New York Times*. "If they were closed today, too, it would have said so on the sign."

She hated to have Kirby see her this way, helpless and incompetent. If only Jarvis had told her what was happening, they could have planned something together. Probably it was her fault that he had felt he couldn't talk to her. Maybe she had nagged and questioned him too much. She had tried to tread carefully, but a man in his position could be hypersensitive.

He might at least have taken them with him. He probably thought they would be safer at home. Damn him, he had never learned to think down here in the real world. He had both feet up in the clouds with Chaucer.

"Oh, damn, damn," she said aloud. "Imagine belonging to a yacht club when you're broke."

Half an hour later she went back to the telephones. She called the restaurant at regular intervals. Finally, at nine-thirty, someone answered.

She felt a wild excitement, which immediately subsided. She did not dare hope for much, but at least this might be the beginning of something.

"Ernie Hampden. Is Mr. Hampden there?"

"He ain't in yet," said the voice.

"When do you expect him?"

"Maybe a hour."

He was still around, then. He existed. He was even expected. She fought an urge to rush downtown and wait for him. But she had wasted a round-trip bus fare yesterday on a futile trip. Something might still go wrong.

She waited an hour and a half. When she dialed again, a woman answered. The woman asked who was calling.

"I'm a relative of his, Pauline Kingsley. It's very, very urgent."

There was a long pause. Then came a softly expelled "Oh," followed by "Just a minute, please."

She heard voices in the background and a crash of something metallic. Restaurant sounds. Then silence as the hold button was pressed.

And suddenly, "Hey, Pauline, how are you? What's up?"

"Ernie! It's really Ernie! I've been trying—I'm in the city, in Grand Central Station, and I can't talk on the phone. It's trouble, Ernie. I'm in big trouble and I can't find anybody I know."

She could imagine what he must be thinking. An abused wife running from home. After a moment, he asked, "Are you alone?"

"My daughter's with me. Not Jarvis. I'll explain all that. I don't want to bother you, but I really don't know what else to do."

"No problem. Why don't you come on over?"

"Thanks. You don't know what this means. I'll be right there."

She was too impatient, and Kirby too tired, for another bus ride. They took a taxi. As they sped down Lexington Avenue, a breeze from the open window blew on their faces and ruffled Kirby's hair.

Pauline watched it ripple in the wind. Pink blond, Jarvis always called it. A distinctive color. With a jolt, she wondered if the thin man who searched their house might have looked into Kirby's room and seen the color of her hair, and remembered it.

But they don't know where we are.

In a few minutes they were climbing out of the taxi in front of Ernie's Steak House. Kirby moaned when they tried the restaurant door and found it locked.

"It's okay," said Pauline. "We're expected." She rapped on the glass pane. The door was opened by a young woman with elaborately coiffed blond hair piled on top of her head. Her blue eyes were cool as they studied Pauline.

"Miss Kingsley?"

69

"Mrs.," said Pauline. "Is Ernie here?"

The woman carefully locked the door and led them through the dining room, down a narrow hallway where the rest rooms were, and into a small office.

Ernie stood up from his desk. He was tall and prematurely bald with a vague, pleasant smile, exactly as she remembered him. When the greetings were over and Kirby had been introduced, Ernie said, "You and Jarvis split up."

"Worse than that." Pauline sat down in a chair next to his desk, ready to tell him everything, beginning with the merger that had cost Jarvis his job.

She had barely started when Ernie said, "Yes, I know."

He seemed uneasy. She thought he might be embarrassed for her.

"He came to see me about a month ago. No, it was more than a month," Ernie explained.

"I didn't know that. I didn't know you were both still in touch."

"He was pretty desperate, I think."

"Don't tell me. He came to borrow money."

"Yes ... well ..."

"When was it, exactly?" she asked.

"Back in May, sometime."

"Near the end of May?"

"Yes, but I couldn't help him. I've got my own troubles, and not much in the way of liquid assets. I'd have had to sell the business."

"Ernie, I can't tell you how glad I am that you didn't do that."

"I could have borrowed against it, maybe."

"Not for Jarvis. He's not a good risk."

70

"Well, he didn't press it, anyway. I could see he felt real uncomfortable about the whole thing."

"Yes. And then he went—oh, God."

"I felt bad, too," Ernie said. "Here was a guy out of work for how long?"

"More than a year."

"I thought he was set for life in that place, Thomas & Flute. He was doing okay."

"Nobody's set for life," she replied, "especially in a thing like publishing. They have turnovers all the time. It wasn't that he was fired, he was just excessed out. It really wasn't fair."

"It happens, though."

"It does, and that's probably why he couldn't find another job. Because there were so many other people in the same boat. He kept looking for work. Anything. I guess he told you all about that."

"No, not much."

"He even applied for clerical jobs. They said he was overqualified. Then he got the cute idea of starting his own publishing company. Did he tell you?"

"That's what he needed the money for, but I couldn't help him. I was pretty impressed, though."

"Don't be. Jarvis is not a businessman. He's bright and creative, but business is a whole separate talent. He couldn't even get rid of the books. If you can't distribute your books, what good are they?"

"It's too bad," said Ernie.

"It wasn't helping our family any. We still had our living expenses and nothing to cover them with."

"How about the house?"

"You know Jarvis wouldn't sell the house. Besides, I

think he took out a mortgage. Now I don't know who's going to pay it and maybe I don't care."

"So what made you run away?"

"The loan sharks."

Ernie looked stricken.

"It's not your fault," she said. "Even if you couldn't help him, we'd have been better off starving. I guess he got out just in time. They came to the house that night. They said if he couldn't pay, it was up to me." She nodded down at Kirby, who was sitting on her lap. "They talked about kids getting hit by a car and falling down old wells. Besides wanting me to be a hooker."

"What about the police? Didn't you tell the police?"

"Of course I did. They couldn't do a thing without evidence."

"Yeah, I guess so. You know, it's hard for me to see Jarvis getting himself mixed up with that. He's a smart boy."

"Man, Ernie, he's a man. I know he's Anne's little brother, but he's twenty-eight years old."

"In some ways. Now, what can I do for you?"

"Well, I've been trying to reach a friend of mine. I thought he could help me get a job where I used to work. The thing is, I need something right away. Kirby and I are down to almost nothing. I was wondering if you might know of a place where I could, you know, get something—"

"Hmmmm." He picked up a pencil and doodled with it.

"I don't dare ask if you need anybody yourself," she said. "But I guess that's really what I'm asking."

He grinned uneasily. "The truth is, I really don't need anybody, but maybe I can use an extra waitress for a while."

72

"No charity, Ernie. I don't want to put you out."

"You call that putting me out? I expect you to earn every cent. When do you want to start? Tomorrow?"

She could not have asked for anything better, but there was still Kirby to think of. She needed a day-care facility.

"A really good, nice place, but not too expensive," she added, "if those terms aren't mutually exclusive."

He went out to consult with his staff and came back accompanied by the blond woman who had admitted them.

"This is Clo," he said. "My partner, cashier, hostess. Also the best scenery we've got around here. Clo Fairweather, Pauline Kingsley."

"Nice to meet you, Clo," said Pauline, starting to offer her hand, and then, at the look on Clo's face, withdrawing it. "I guess I'm a former sister-in-law. I was asking Ernie about a day-care place for my little girl."

Kirby, who had been nearly asleep, woke with a start. Pauline patted her reassuringly.

"There's a place not too far from here," Clo replied. "One of our girls took her kid there. It's called Happy—Happy Hour. Something like that.

"She was not sure of the name and didn't know the address. It's on Twenty-fifth Street. It has a red door and the name's on the door."

As Clo left the room, Pauline stared after her, dazed. "It's happening so fast," she said to Ernie. "I waited all night, and now it's happening so fast I can't believe it. There were three things I needed, and this makes two of them already."

"What's the third?" he asked.

"A place to live. But that's not so easy, is it?"

"Not in this town. I'd like to help you, but my apartment's very small. It wouldn't be comfortable. There's a place a couple of blocks from here that sometimes rents out rooms."

"An SRO building?"

"It's a little better than that. It's a single-room occupancy, but not the kind you usually think of. I can't guarantee they'll have anything."

He cleared the papers from a plastic-covered couch and they transferred the sleeping Kirby to it. Kirby woke and began to cry.

"It's all right, baby, I'm coming right back," Pauline promised. "I just want to find us a place to live."

The rooming house, a well-kept Victorian brownstone, had no vacancies.

"You can put your name on the waiting list, if you want," the elderly landlady told her indifferently.

"How long is the waiting list?"

"About eight or ten. But a lot of times they find something else."

Pauline put down her name with the restaurant's address and phone number. Two out of three. At least they wouldn't have to sleep in the park again. There was Ernie's couch, if nothing else.

She walked south to Twenty-fifth Street and looked for a red door. Clo had not even known which block it was on. She searched back and forth from Madison Avenue to Second before she realized that the door was part of a church and the name on it was not Happy Hour but Merry Days Play Center.

She was dismayed at the cost and intrigued by the playground in back of the school. She did not think she could do better, and nothing, no matter how expensive, was too good for Kirby.

The director, a motherly woman named Mrs. Vogel, told her the enrollment was full.

Pauline's mouth opened. "What am I going to do?"

Mrs. Vogel studied the top of her desk for a while, then rocked back in her swivel chair.

"I don't like to give the teachers more than they can handle," she said. "We've got two who are young and just starting here, and if they're overloaded, it's not good for the children. But you do seem anxious. Maybe we can make an exception. We open at eight in the morning and close at six. You don't have to be here at eight if your hours are later, but we do ask that the children be picked up by six."

"How about earlier? I finish work at four."

"Preferably not earlier. We keep to a schedule in the afternoon."

"I see," said Pauline. "And thank you for helping us."

On her way back to the restaurant she tried again to call Dudley. There was still no answer. She stopped at a hotel and inquired about the rates. A room for one or two nights, she discovered, would probably wipe out her week's pay.

By the time she returned, the restaurant had opened for lunch and Ernie was busy. She waited for him in the back office, sitting in the chair next to his desk and contemplating her sleeping daughter. Her own head felt heavy. Cobwebby. She couldn't pull her thoughts together, and doubted that she would ever be able to get up out of the chair. Her eyes were beginning to close when Ernie came in.

"How did it go?" he asked.

"I got the school but not the room. There's a waiting list. I even tried a hotel, but that's out of the question. Do you know of any other places around here? An agency, maybe?"

"An agency wouldn't get you anything you could afford," he said. "I'm not surprised you struck out. This city's pretty impossible for housing. If you do find something, it'd be too steep. Looks like it'll have to be my place for a while."

"Really, Ernie, I don't want to cause you any more trouble. We'll be happy to sleep on the floor. Here or anywhere."

He grinned. "At my place it probably will be the floor, since that's what I've got. But I want you to understand, it's a very small apartment and there's already two of us."

"Oh, you're remarried?"

"Not exactly. It's Clo, the girl you met."

"The blonde? She's very attractive. But won't she mind?"

"I'll talk to her," he said.

"I asked if she'd mind."

He took a deep breath and let it out. "No, she won't mind. I'll take you over there and get you settled. But have some lunch first."

9

He had tried several times to call her. He couldn't believe she wasn't there. Always it was the damned answering machine, and always the same cryptic message.

"I'm sorry you can't reach us right now. As soon as I can, I'll try to get a message to you through your last address. You know the one I mean. I'll explain then."

"Damn!" he said, hanging up the receiver. He was in a diner somewhere in central New York State. The phone booth was stifling, but he didn't want to leave it. He didn't want to give up again.

His fingers drummed on the shelf below the phone. He knew what it all meant. He couldn't help knowing.

They had gotten to her. He wanted to think she had left because he had run out on her, but it wasn't that. She wouldn't have had to encode her message. Or leave any at all. Because she would have gone to her parents, but the message was for them. She had had to bolt. And it was his fault.

Where would she go? He had left her a hundred dollars. He didn't know how much else she had. He didn't know how far she could go with it.

From the message, he gathered that she couldn't find her parents. So it had to be one of her friends. Her best friend was Sue Rhinehart. He couldn't remember the number. Damn it, all he had in his address book were his own business friends, acquaintances, people he had worked with, people he hoped to work with.

He called Information and got the Rhineharts' number, but no one answered. It didn't mean anything. They could all have gone out. Would they go out on Tuesday afternoon? Not if she was trying to lie low.

He couldn't remember who her friends were in New York. That woman, the one at the magazine—she had gotten married, too. He hadn't the faintest idea what her married name was.

And there was a man. Jarvis remembered his voice, precise and fruity. He could not remember what the man looked like. As for his name, all he could think of was Dudley Moore, which came to mind so easily that he was sure it wasn't right.

"Damn," he said again. It was all his fault. Maybe they had kidnapped her and forced her to record the message.

He went out to the counter and ordered a cup of coffee, partly to get more change and partly to clear his head. He was tired, that was part of the trouble. He drank the coffee and looked through his address book. All those useless contacts. What had they done for him? He had lost everything now, even his wife and daughter.

Several hundred miles to go. He didn't know how many hundred, and there wasn't time to count them. He would get home and maybe she would be there. Or

78

maybe he would find a clue as to where she had gone.

Or maybe the Broker and his friends would be there, waiting. Maybe it was all a trap. They were holding her prisoner. Now they were waiting for him.

A few more hours. A few hundred miles. You couldn't go a hundred miles an hour. Which would be used up first, the hours or the miles?

He shook his head. He had almost fallen asleep and his thoughts didn't make any sense.

He went out to the car and started driving again, and he couldn't stop. There was no time to rest. For miles, he saw nothing but fields. Farmhouses. He couldn't go in and ask some farm wife for a cup of coffee.

And then another village. He headed toward the commercial part of it. Even that was not very commercial Hardly more than a few tacky stores. How did people live in a place like that?

He went on to the next town. It was larger, thank God. He saw the sign far beyond the Exxon and the Mobil. A Burger King. At the drive-in window he ordered another coffee, and a large Coke for the road. Coke had caffeine, too, and it was cold. He needed that.

Ten minutes later, he was on his way again. It had been a brief interlude. All too brief. He waited for the coffee to take effect.

After a while he began to feel it, but not in his head. He should have used the rest room at Burger King. It didn't matter, really. With the summer foliage out, he could stop anywhere.

Maybe he would find a telephone and try calling Pauline again. And Sue Rhinehart. Failing those, maybe Pennikan, his father's lawyer. Could you ask a lawyer to go

79

check on your house, your wife? Probably not, unless you paid him a retainer. All Pennikan had done for Jarvis personally was draw up a will, and that had been four years ago, when Kirby was born. Now there was nothing to leave her, poor kid.

He drove on and on, his only satisfaction being the miles he was covering, before he found a gas station. It was the first one he had seen in all that time. He had to stop, in spite of the two old cars full of rowdy young people with blaring radios. Generally he tried to avoid such scenes. They made him uneasy. It probably meant that he was getting old. He filled his tank, then drove over and parked on the side, near a glassed-in telephone booth.

He dialed his home number. Again he heard the message. He listened to her voice and then hung up.

Sue Rhinehart didn't answer, either. He dialed Pennikan's office. The lawyer was in court. Jarvis considered trying to explain his whole story to the secretary. It seemed insurmountably difficult.

"Thanks. No, no message." After he hung up he wished he had left a message, but he wouldn't have known what to say.

He crossed the pavement, which radiated heat like an electric grill, and entered the men's room. It was a small, grimy cubicle. He locked himself in. With his pants unzipped and an unstoppable stream heading for the urinal, he heard a car start up.

The hairs rose on the back of his neck. He didn't know why.

Because the engine sounded familiar. A guy gets to know the sound of his own engine.

They couldn't have hot wired it that fast, he thought as he patted his pocket. The pocket into which he usually slipped his keys.

It was empty.

And then he remembered that he had left the keys in the ignition because the car was right outside the phone booth and he could see it, and—oh, hell.

He stopped the stream and zipped his pants. He had to be wrong. How much did a guy have to take?

He opened the door and, for a moment, almost saw the ghost of his car by the phone booth, he wanted it so badly.

10

Pauline could see what Ernie meant about the size of his apartment. It had one small bedroom, which was nearly filled with a double bed, and a living room furnished almost entirely with large cushions.

"We can make a bed out of these," he said, meaning the cushions. "On the other hand, we'll be coming home late. Maybe you should have the bedroom."

"No, please, Ernie, we can sleep anywhere. The cushions look marvelous."

He gave her an extra set of keys and went back to the restaurant.

"A bed!" she exclaimed when he had left. "Do you know Mommy hasn't slept for two nights?"

They arranged the cushions and the bedding Ernie had provided, and lay down.

Hours later they were awakened by the sound of the doorbell. It was one of Ernie's busboys bringing over a dinner of fried chicken.

After eating, Pauline showered and washed her hair,

then fell again into a dreamless sleep.

She woke to lights and voices when Ernie and Clo arrived home. They went directly into the bedroom. She heard a door close, but their voices came through the wall.

"Okay, but I hope you're not going to keep her long."

"Will you shut up?" Ernie sounded angry. What could it take to make Ernie angry?

"Of all the dumb things, when we're already having trouble."

"I told you—" The voices faded.

Then Clo again. "And this place is cramped enough."

"Keep it quiet, will you? It's only for—"

She could hear mumbling, but could not make out the words.

Go back—but they'll find me. And I need a job....

She drifted, seeing dreamlike images, and then she slept.

The next morning at nine o'clock, before Ernie and Clo were awake, she walked Kirby to the Merry Days Play Center.

"I hate to do this, baby, but Mommy has to work. I'll be right nearby at Uncle Ernie's restaurant. He really is sort of your uncle, did you know that? He used to be married to your Aunt Anne."

They told her Kirby would be all right. She left, hearing Kirby's heartbroken sobs. *Damn you, Jarvis.*

Kirby would be all right. She attended nursery school in Allenbury. It was nothing new to her.

Pauline walked north and then east along tree-shaded sidewalks, past picturesque shops and restaurants. She

83

would find an apartment and a better job, and Kirby would adjust. For now, it was enough just to be back in the city. Allenbury was behind them.

She reached Dudley's building and found his mailbox empty. Elated, she pressed the doorbell.

After a minute, she rang again. And again. It had been too much to hope for. She had had her share of good luck yesterday.

Back outside, she strolled along the street. She was early yet for the restaurant, and did not want to barge in on Ernie and Clo. She headed downtown toward the play school, which was only four blocks out of her way. It was a clear sunny morning, and she was finally free to enjoy her life again.

She walked slowly past the school, feeling Kirby's presence there. From the sidewalk she could not see anyone inside, but she heard their voices, occasional shouts and squeals. She hoped Kirby had gotten over her fear and was making new friends. It wrenched her to leave the child in that place with so little preparation, after the upheavals of the past few days.

Can it, she told herself. *You can't afford to feel guilty. Only if there's a choice.*

As she waited to cross the avenue, a long black car slid up behind her. She turned to look at it, and felt her heart begin to pound. Just because it was a long black car? She could not see through the tinted glass windows. Anybody could have tinted windows. The car turned up the avenue, and when she reached the next block, she saw it again on the street to the north of her.

She began to walk quickly, purposefully. She would not let anything sneak up on her again.

84

At the next block she met Ernie. He saw her coming and greeted her with a pleasant, easygoing smile.

"It's a small town after all, isn't it?" she said.

"Small town?"

"Running into each other like this."

"Yeah, well, we're both going to the same place at the same time. Only you don't need to come so early."

"I have nothing else to do. Where's Clo?"

"She went on ahead to start things going."

"Is she really your partner?" Pauline asked. "I thought it was all your own business."

"It was, originally. She's not a full partner. Last year it needed a transfusion. New cash. Clo had some money, so we got together."

"That's a pretty name, Clo Fairweather."

"Stage name. Her real name's Feeney."

"She was in show business?"

"For a while. She didn't do too well. It's rough out there. A rough business, and she was married to a guy who liked to gamble. She needed something steady. Got a job as a cocktail waitress."

"Is that better?"

"It's steadier."

"What did you mean about your business needing new cash? Were you having trouble?"

"Still am. It's a funny thing. You ever notice what an ethnic town this is?"

"Not really," she said. "But I haven't been here in a while."

"Sure it's ethnic. When people go out, it's always 'Do you want French food? Italian food? Chinese food?' In this neighborhood we've got a lot of Armenian restaurants. We've got Lebanese, Breton, French. Everything's French. You gotta offer something special."

"Well, you do. You're a steak house."

"I don't know. It seems like you have to be ethnic, even if it's only Chinese or Italian. There's one on practically every block."

"Ernie, that can't be true. I mean, that you have to be Chinese or Italian."

"I don't know, maybe it's the cooking, but something's wrong. I was trying to think of something different. The trouble is, I'm not different. When you're a WASP, what are you? A WASP is sort of negative. It's the absence of anything else."

"That's what I used to think of vanilla ice cream," she said. "But I finally discovered vanilla's a flavor, too."

"A lot of people don't think it's a very interesting one. But Jarvis gave me an idea. Maybe I owe him something for that."

"You already paid him. You're taking care of us. What was his idea?"

"Chavakovi's Original Belsorbian Restaurant."

"What?"

"It came off the top of his head. He must be good at that sort of thing. I'm planning to revamp the whole place. Can't you just see all the waiters in boots and cummerbunds, and the girls with fluffy blouses and ribbons? And we'll have stuff on flaming swords ..."

"You're not serious about this."

"Dead serious. All I need is the money for redecorating. I applied for a loan."

"But it's crazy. It sounds like the sort of thing Jarvis would do. What does Clo think?"

86

"She thinks it's crazy, too, but she agrees we have to do something."

When they reached the restaurant, he led her around to the side street and unlocked the service entrance. It opened into a corridor next to the kitchen, where the cooks were already at work.

Clo, who had been conferring with the head chef, came toward them, her face set in small lines when she saw them together.

"You realize," she said to Ernie, "we'll have to change the waitress stations."

"Why, is somebody sick?"

"No, because we have an extra waitress."

"Okay, you go ahead and change them."

Pauline murmured, "I'm sorry, Ernie." She did not think he heard her. Clo gave her a red apron to wear over her requisite white blouse and black skirt, and briefed her on the procedure.

When the restaurant opened for lunch, Pauline mixed up her first order. She was lectured by Clo and consoled by another waitress, who assured her that she would get used to it.

During a lull after the lunchtime rush, Pauline slipped out to a pay phone in the hall by the rest rooms. She dialed Dudley's number, closed her eyes when the ringing began, and opened them with a start when it broke off.

"Dudley? Dudley?"

"Who is this?"

"Pauline Kingsley. I tried to call you."

"Right! I returned your call. You weren't there."

"I'm in the city now. I've been calling you every hour."

"Trouble, huh? You left your husband?"

87

"It's the other way around, but there was a reason. I can't talk about it on the phone. Can I see you?"

"Sure. Where are you staying?"

"Nowhere. I'm sleeping on somebody's floor, but he has a girlfriend. It's awkward. Anyhow, I'm working as a waitress. I get off at four. It's not far from you."

"Hey, terrific! Do you want to meet somewhere, or come here?"

"I don't want to bother you . . ."

"Not at all. I just got back from Bermuda and I don't start my new job till Monday. Your place or mine?"

"How about your place? I can relax there. What's your new job?"

"Public relations. A friend of mine has an outfit. See you about four-thirty?"

From the cashier's desk, Clo watched Pauline come in from the rest room, smiling to herself. Clo rang up a customer's change and added more toothpicks to the cup on the desk. A tableful of businessmen came over to pay their bill. She pushed forward the basket of advertising matches. They should all remember Ernie's restaurant.

"Have a nice day," she told them cheerily, "and come again soon."

They had spent half the afternoon there, sitting and smoking, taking up the whole table, but people like that were valuable customers. They usually came back and they always spent money like it didn't belong to them, which it didn't. She took a mint and put it into her mouth, savoring the crumbling sweetness.

The telephone rang. She reached for it absentmindedly as she brushed a fly away from the mints.

"Clo, baby, how are you doing?"

"Just fine, how are you?" She tried to identify the voice.

"Listen, honey. That guy from Connecticut you sent over."

Recognition jolted through her.

"What about him?"

"He skipped, baby. He's gone."

"Yeah? That's too bad." She had to act surprised.

"That's too bad," mimicked the voice. "Aren't you missing something, Clo?"

"What do you mean."

"The guy borrowed forty grand. That's a lot of cash."

"Yeah, it is."

"Forty grand," the voice repeated. "Plus there's two grand a week. I don't have to tell you, honey. Five percent, remember? Your friend missed two weeks already. Payment's due tomorrow. That's the third week."

"Yes? Well?" Her fingers gripped the telephone stickily.

"You sent him, Clo."

"He needed the money. I knew where he could get it. I didn't know he was going to run out on you. I don't even know the guy, really. He just came to see a friend of mine."

"Clo, baby, you know how it works."

"What are you talking about?"

"You sent the guy. He skips and you're responsible."

She could not believe what she was hearing. "That's not fair!"

"What's fair? You think I should take the loss?"

"But—why me?"

"Because you're the one that recommended him."

"I didn't recommend *him*, I recommended *you*. I don't even know him."

"You know me, don't you? Who saved your neck that time in Atlantic City?"

"I paid it all back!"

"Sure you paid it back. You won big."

"I paid back everything I owed you."

"And bought into that business."

"This business has nothing to do with you or your money. Hang on a minute."

She pressed the hold button so he wouldn't hear the ring of the cash register as she made change for a customer. It was impossible to concentrate on what she was doing. She tried to think of a way out before she resumed the conversation. It didn't matter whether or not she thought it was fair. If that was the way they did things, you couldn't fight it.

She opened the line again.

"What about the man's wife? Why isn't she responsible for his debt? Why me?"

"She's gone," he replied. "The both of them, they're gone. They think it's some kind of game."

"They don't think it's a game. That's why they're gone. And I know where the wife is. She's right here. She took the kid and came here. She knows my friend from way back. He gave her a job."

"The hell you say."

He spoke slowly and the s was drawn out, or maybe it was a defect in the telephone connection. It made her think of rattlesnakes.

90

11

Dudley wore a T-shirt with a rip under one arm. His face was unshaven.

"What happened to your old dapper self?" Pauline asked.

He grinned apologetically. "Sorry. I'm still on vacation. What can I offer you? Gin and tonic?"

"That would be perfect." She sat down on a green brocaded sofa in a gentle breeze from the air conditioner and slipped off her shoes. It was not exactly home at last, but it was gradually getting there.

He mixed the drink and handed it to her. "Now tell me your troubles. All of them."

She did not have to begin at the beginning. Dudley knew about Jarvis's unemployment. She told of the publishing venture and the catastrophic losses. He shook his head and clicked his tongue. She told about waking up to find Jarvis gone, and the two men from the loan shark.

"That was when I called you. I had to get away so they couldn't find me, and I didn't know where to go or what to do."

"Why didn't you just call the police?"

It really was an obvious question. She explained once again about the police.

"So then I started calling people. I can't count the number of times I tried to get you. First I got your answering machine, and then it just rang. I thought you were back, but when I came over here, your mailbox was full."

"Yes, something happened with the machine. It stopped hooking into the phone system. Everything else works fine." Dudley's rubber *zori* slapped across the floor. For all the size of his apartment, the kitchen was only an alcove. He came back with a bowl of salted nuts and set it on the rosewood cocktail table, pushing aside an expensive art book.

"I didn't get in till late last night," he added, "and I called you first thing, but you weren't there."

"I came over this morning and rang your doorbell."

"Sorry about that. I wear earplugs when I want a good night's sleep. Now let's see, who are you staying with?"

"Jarvis's sister's ex-husband. He's the only person I could find, but there's no room in his apartment."

"Why don't you stay here? I've got plenty of room. You wouldn't even have to sleep on the floor. That's a pull-out sofa."

"Dudley, you do understand that I have my little girl."

"Of course. There's room for both of you. It's a double."

It was what she had hoped for, but hadn't dared suggest. It would be so much easier than imposing on Ernie, whom she did not know as well.

92

"That's lovely, Dudley. I hope it won't be for long. I really want to find my own place."

"It'll take a while. I'll ask around for you. And a job, too. I assume you want to work in an office. How about another drink?"

She held out her glass and he refilled it. Every few minutes she checked her watch.

"If you want, I can set an alarm for you," he teased.

"I'm sorry. It's her first day there, and we've been through a lot. I want to be sure she's okay. They said she has to be picked up by six, but not before, which doesn't give much leeway."

She studied his gray-blue eyes fringed with long dark lashes. His neatly combed gray hair. It suited him, that gray. He could not have been more than thirty-five and his face was still young, but for as long as she had known him, he had had gray hair.

She began to cry.

"You just don't know," she sobbed, "how good it is to see you again. To be here. To be someplace where it's safe."

"Oh, dear girl, it's not that bad." He was clearly uneasy. "I thought the drink would make you happy."

"It's going to take a lot more than a drink to make me happy, but I didn't mean this part of it's bad. It's what came before."

She, too, was embarrassed by her outburst. She sipped her drink and tried to compose herself.

Dudley asked, "Where do you think Jarvis might have gone?"

"I don't know. Maybe his sister in California. I'm not even sure I care."

"Yes, but he's responsible for all this."

"He is. He got me into it, but I don't need him to get me out. I seem to be doing all right, with a lot of help from other people." She glanced at her watch. It was a quarter to six.

"Couldn't you try calling his sister?"

"Dudley, I don't know if I want to talk to him. I'd probably just kill him." She set down her glass. "Time to get going. Do you feel like walking over there with me?"

"Well, uh—" He rubbed his cheek. "I'd have to shave first."

"You really don't, you know. A lot of people go around like that."

"Not me. I'd feel sloppy. If you care to wait, I can do it pretty fast, but you said you had to leave."

"I really think I'd better. It's her first day."

"And you'll come back here?"

"If it's okay with you."

He walked with her out to the elevator. As it closed, she blew him a kiss. "See you!"

Downstairs, she pulled open the heavy, locked front door and then the outer glass door. She barely noticed the sleek gray car at the curb. It had nothing to do with her—until its door opened and the fat man stepped out.

In a hazy dream, she watched him come toward her. "Mrs. Kingsley?"

She paused, frozen, her brain still foggy from the gin. *How did they find me?* She plunged back into the building. Frantically, she rang the doorbell and rattled the latch to the inner door. Over her shoulder she glimpsed the fat man on the sidewalk, his arms folded, watching her.

94

Finally, Dudley's voice crackled through the intercom. "Who is it? Pauline?"

"Yes! Let me in!"

The release buzzer sounded and she pushed open the door. She forced it closed behind her and ran up the stairs, not waiting for the elevator.

Dudley stood in his open doorway.

"They're down there!" she gasped.

"What? Who?"

"Those men. They're down there. In front of the building." She tried to catch her breath. "I thought they were going to grab me. And I have to get—have to get Kirby. What am I going to do?"

He opened one of his front windows and looked out. "That gray car?"

"Yes. Is he still out there? The man? Don't let him see you."

Dudley withdrew and closed the window. "I don't know if he saw me. There are two of them. One's in the car."

"What am I going to do?"

"I'll go with you. Just wait a sec." He went into the bathroom. *How could he think of shaving?*

"But they'll follow us," she said. "They'll know where to find her."

"Maybe you should call the school and tell them you'll be a little late."

"They could stay there all night. Isn't there a back way out?"

"Only a courtyard. There's no way out to the street."

Through the open bathroom door she could see him in the mirror, lathering his face. She rubbed her forehead. The hazy gin feeling had gone, but she couldn't think.

The school. She had to call the school.

"Where do you keep your phone book?"

"On the table by the door. Do you want me to go and get her? They wouldn't know me, and you could stay here."

"She wouldn't know you either, and I told her never to go with anybody else. Besides, I think I should be there. It's her first day."

"You should have a code word," he suggested. "Then, if you have to send somebody, they could give the code. If they don't know it, she wouldn't go with them."

"It's too late now." She turned the pages of the phone book. H. Happy Hour. That wasn't it.

Merry Hour. Merry Christmas. She turned to the M's. Merry Days.

"It's not here!"

"That book's about a year old. The new ones should be coming out. Try Information."

It took her a moment to remember the digits for Directory Assistance. She asked for the Merry Hour Nursery School. Her head began to ache.

"Would that be the Merry Days Play Center?" the operator inquired.

"Yes, that's it. Oh, God." She wrote down the number. "I can't believe all this."

She dialed and heard it ring. Six. Seven. Eight times. Dudley finished his shaving and went into the bedroom.

"No answer?" he called.

"They can't all be gone. Hello?"

It was a soft voice, not Mrs. Vogel's. Pauline identified herself.

"My daughter, Kirby, just started there this morning. I was on my way to pick her up, but something happened. I can't come right now. I'll get there as soon as I can."

"Well, you know, the school closes at six."

"Yes, but I can't *get* there. I'm really sorry. If someone could just take care of her . . ."

"What did you say her name is?"

"Kirby Kingsley. She's four years old."

"Most of the children have already left," said the voice.

"Kirby can't have left, because I'm not there to pick her up. Could you please just keep her until I get there?"

Of course they would keep her. What else would they do with her? Again the voice mumbled something about the school closing.

Dudley came out of the bedroom, buttoning a clean sports shirt. He went to the window and looked again.

"Still there," he reported. "We'll give it five."

"And then what?"

"Then we'll think of something."

"They don't seem to want to keep the school open," Pauline said. "Do you think they'd take her to the police station if I didn't get there? Would they do something intelligent like that?"

"What did you give as your address."

"Ernie's apartment. But nobody will be there till late tonight."

She felt helpless and angry. Tears came into her eyes and she turned away to hide them.

He offered her another drink.

She shook her head. "I didn't mean to fall apart. It's just that I worry about her. And damn it, I feel persecuted."

"Well, you are."

"You're right. I wasn't trying to get out of paying the debt. They scared me away. Any normal person would have worked out some kind of arrangement, or maybe threatened me with a lawyer, which I could handle, but they threatened my child's life."

"That's normal for them, I suppose." He splashed some gin into his empty glass and drank it.

She settled back on the sofa and tried to relax. It was a cool, beautiful apartment, exquisitely furnished. Too well-kept for a child, but Kirby was not a rowdy child.

"Did you mean it about letting us stay here? I know we'll be in your way. At least your place is a little bigger than Ernie's, and—you don't have a girlfriend, do you?"

"Nope." He set his glass down in the kitchen sink and turned to her with a complacent smile. "I never had a girlfriend."

"Oh." She had wondered about it, but hadn't known for sure. "Maybe that's one reason I feel so at ease with you."

"Possibly. Or maybe it's just my charm." He went to look out of the window again. This time he turned to her, smiling.

"The car's gone."

"Is it really?" She hurried over to see for herself. She looked up and down the block, checking every car.

"Dudley, they're gone!" She glanced at her watch. "It's almost six-thirty."

Dudley pocketed his keys and they went out to the elevator. As they left the building, she surveyed the street once more. They really were gone. But now they knew where she was. They would find her again when they

98

wanted her.

"Maybe I was stupid," she said, "panicking like that. Maybe he just wanted to talk, but somehow I don't think talking's their thing. Do you realize he must have been following me since yesterday?"

In the park, they had been so vulnerable. He could have approached them in the park while Kirby slept.

Dudley asked, "Is there any way they could have gotten into your house?"

"Sure. All they'd have to do is pick the lock or break a window. Why?"

"Well, when I returned your call, I left my name and number. I always do, but if I'd known what the problem was, I could have skipped the number. Now, damn it, it's all recorded on your answering machine."

"You think they got your number from my machine?"

"It would be perfectly simple, if they got into your house. Then they could trace me through the phone company, or even the book. I left my last name, too. After all, you might know ten Dudleys. So I suppose they've been watching the building, assuming you'd show up."

"They wouldn't even have to break into the house," she said. "They wouldn't have to do anything. I couldn't find the remote key for that machine and I thought Jarvis took it. But one of them searched the house and he probably got it."

"Oh, hell. After all you did to lose them. What can I say?"

"It's not your fault, Dudley. How could you know? I just should have done that thing with the police, but I was scared."

"Of course you were. It's risky. And you had the kid to think about."

"I wish I could have done it. But I'm scared even now. I'd probably break out in a sweat, or start shaking, and give myself away."

They crossed the street to the block where the school was. She looked down toward the church. No one was standing about on the sidewalk. There were no mothers chatting, no young children at all.

Because it was late. Very late. She hurried past the privet hedge and up the walk. The red door was closed.

She tugged at the knob.

"It's locked," she said.

Dudley tried the knob. They knocked on the door and listened. She pounded with her fist. Then she noticed a doorbell and rang it. Inside, they heard a faint, faraway peal. She rang the bell again and waited.

12

"Where is she? What did they do with her? They couldn't just—" She pounded again on the red door, and rang the bell.

"Maybe one of the teachers took her home," Dudley suggested.

"I shouldn't have been late. Her first day." She had a vision of Kirby, round-eyed and frightened, dragged off by a stranger to a strange apartment.

"Maybe there's somebody in the church."

They went up the steps to the church entrance. It, too, was locked. She tugged first at one heavy brass handle and then the other.

Dudley hammered on the door. "Anybody there?"

A moment later they heard a sound inside. A woman's voice asked, "Who is it?"

Pauline replied, "I'm trying to find someone from the nursery school. They've all gone and I can't find my child."

"Come around to the side door," the woman said.

There was a small door between the nursery school and the main entrance. It had a peephole in it. They heard a click at the peephole, and then the door was unlatched.

The woman who admitted them was small and gray-haired.

"You're looking for someone from the school? I think they've all gone home."

"Yes, I realize that," Pauline said, "but somebody must have my daughter, or know where she is. Do you know where I can reach them? Mrs. Vogel or somebody?"

"I can give you Mrs. Vogel's number. Come on into the office. You can use the phone there. You understand, the school's not affiliated with us. They just rent the space."

The woman led them into a small, cluttered office with leaded windows. She spun a Rolodex file until she found the right card, then turned it toward Pauline.

Mrs. Vogel could offer no enlightenment. "I wasn't aware of any problem. I just assumed she went home like all the other children."

"But she couldn't have," said Pauline, "because I couldn't get there to pick her up. I called the school and told them, and asked if they could keep her for a while."

"Who did you talk to?"

"I don't know. She sounded young and not too sure of herself."

"Probably my secretary. She didn't say anything to me, so she must have thought everything was all right. I'll give Kirby's teacher a call, but I doubt if she's home yet. Where can I reach you?"

Pauline gave her the location and the number, and settled down to wait on a bench outside the office. Dudley said, "She'll be all right. I'm sure the teacher has her, or took her somewhere."

"Then I should be at Ernie's. That's what I put for my address and phone number."

He patted her hand. "Just sit tight. You don't want to confuse them any worse."

Twenty minutes later Mrs. Vogel called back. "I'm still trying to get Kirby's teacher."

"Thank you," Pauline said dully. She pictured the teacher on an endless train ride to Far Rockaway or northern Westchester. She imagined a stiff, straight woman, grudgingly taking charge of a small child with pink-gold hair and a mouth turned down in misery.

"What if she's not all right?"

"Don't borrow trouble, darling." Dudley stood up and began to pace the floor. "Would you like some coffee? I can go out and get something."

"No, thank you."

She wanted oblivion, not coffee.

"I shouldn't have left her here. I don't know what I could have done, but she was so afraid. I wish I'd taken her home."

She kept seeing Kirby, her last glimpse of Kirby as she had left her that morning, sad, frightened, and alone.

She tried instead to think of their reunion. Even if she had to travel to the far end of Brooklyn or Staten Island, it wouldn't matter, as long as Kirby was safe.

Why wouldn't she be safe? The very word, with its implied alternative, was chilling.

After a while the telephone rang and the secretary called her again.

It was Mrs. Vogel.

"I just talked to Miss Rose. She says Kirby was picked up at six o'clock by her uncle."

"Uncle!" exclaimed Pauline. "Ernie? But he wouldn't—Did she call him? Because I was late?"

"She didn't say whether she called him," Mrs. Vogel replied. "She just said Kirby's uncle picked her up at six."

Six was when she was supposed to have been picked up. It was not because Pauline was late.

"Listen, this is important. Do you mind holding on while I call my brother-in-law?"

She did not wait for an answer. She pressed the hold button and dialed the restaurant.

"Clo? Is Ernie there? This is Pauline. I have to know whether he picked up Kirby at school."

There was no immediate answer. "Clo?" she prompted.

Clo said, "Picked up Kirby? Why would he do that?"

"She's missing. They said her uncle picked her up. He's the only sort of uncle she has. Please let me talk to him."

Clo mumbled something, and she heard the deadness of the hold button. *Please. Please let her be there.*

Ernie came on the line. "Hi, what's up? Kirby missing?"

"You don't have her? Ernie, they said her uncle picked her up at school. If you didn't, then who did?"

"It wasn't me. I figured you were meeting her. Do you think Jarvis could have come back, maybe?"

"Jarvis! How would he know where she is? And why would he say he's her uncle? I think something's hap-

104

pened. I think—" She broke the connection and returned to Mrs. Vogel.

"Listen, I just talked to Kirby's uncle and he doesn't know anything about it. There's nobody else who even knew where she was. Please give me the number of that teacher. I have to talk to her directly."

"I'll tell Miss Rose what you said and—"

"I want to talk to her myself! Don't you understand? This is serious! There's a good chance my child was kidnapped while she was in your care."

"I'll have her call you right away," Mrs. Vogel said. "But please understand, Miss Rose is young and rather inexp—"

"I don't give a *damn*." Pauline hung up the phone.

She looked over at the secretary, who was staring at her in alarmed fascination. "I'm sorry to tie up your phone like this."

"It's no problem at all," the woman chirped. "I just hope your child is all right."

The phone rang under Pauline's hand. The secretary answered and handed it to her.

"This is Rose Lipson. There was a man waiting for Kirby and he said he was her uncle."

"Well, he wasn't! Didn't Kirby say he wasn't?"

"She didn't say anything. She just went with him. He had a woman there. I thought it might be you."

"I told her not to go with strangers! She should have said something."

Kirby, Kirby, it's not your fault.

What else could she have expected from Kirby, after all the changes and craziness of the past few days? A four-year-old, afraid to argue with an adult.

105

"What did he look like? Just tell me what he looked like."

"He was sort of medium. He had dark hair."

Her hands, holding the telephone, began to tremble.

"Miss whatever your name is," she screamed, "don't you know any better than to do a thing like that?"

"Well, you see, I never met you, and—"

"And now she's been kidnapped! And they're going to kill her! They said they'd kill her because her father owes them money."

Sobbing, she slammed down the phone.

An arm went around her. A brotherly hug.

"Pauline, darling, don't you think it's time for the police?"

"I don't know. I don't know what to do."

"That's the logical thing. They've had a lot more experience with, uh—"

"Oh God, Dudley!"

"We'll go back to my place and call them." He looked over at the bug-eyed secretary. "Thanks for everything."

"I sure hope you find her," she said.

"Thank you," Pauline murmured. Dudley took her elbow and led her outside.

"Oh, my God," she moaned. "Oh, God."

"That's why they were there," he said. "That was probably a set-up, when you left my building. They just wanted to stop you one way or another until they got hold of Kirby."

She began to cry again. "What am I going to do?"

"You could use another gin and tonic. I'll be fixing it while you call the police."

"I think I want to call Ernie. Right now."

106

She was not sure why. Common sense would not let her admit the nagging hope that maybe she had heard him wrong, or he had misunderstood her. That maybe Kirby was there after all.

At the next corner she found a pay phone and called the restaurant.

Again Clo answered. "Oh, Pauline, is that you? Did you find her?"

"No, I didn't," Pauline said hollowly.

"There was a phone call for you a little while ago."

"At the restaurant? Who was it?"

"A man. He wouldn't leave a message. Not even his name."

"Oh, Clo. Oh, my God. I'll be right there. Are they going to call again?"

"He didn't say. If he does, I'll tell him you're coming."

She turned from the telephone. Her body felt numb.

"They called the restaurant. I'm going there to wait."

"I'll go with you," Dudley said. "Darling, I can't tell you how sorry I am."

The restaurant was cool and quiet, with expanses of white tablecloth on unoccupied tables. Although it was prime time for dinner, the place was only half filled. She barely noticed it as Clo hurried toward her.

"You poor thing," Clo exclaimed. "I'm sure they'll call again. Just tell me where you're going to be, and I'll get you on the phone right away."

Pauline told her she would be in the office, if it was all right with Ernie.

Dudley wrote down the police number for her.

"Now, how about a drink?" he said. "I'll go out to the bar."

"No, thanks. I couldn't swallow."

She dialed the number he had written for her. The police tried to calm her, assuring her that it was probably a mistake.

"Mistake?" she repeated. "Somebody mistook my child for their own?"

She told about the loan shark and the threats. About the events of that evening. It seemed stupid, now that she knew the outcome, to have been frightened away by a fat man, but he would have detained her somehow.

"And the man who picked her up said he was her uncle, but she hasn't got an uncle."

"Okay, we'll have somebody there in a couple of minutes."

Exactly what they had said in Connecticut. They couldn't protect her, and now it had happened.

Please, God, don't punish her.

Dudley came back with a gin and tonic for each of them. She took hers reluctantly, knowing she couldn't drink it.

Then Ernie was there, hugging her and patting her shoulder.

"Terrible," he said. "It's just terrible. Maybe we should have kept her here in my office. I didn't think—"

"Neither did I," said Pauline. "And she'd have been bored here. The school was supposed to take care of her. I can't understand the teacher just letting her go off with somebody. I thought they weren't supposed to do that."

"They'll probably give her hell, and you should, too. Get a lawyer."

She nodded. She couldn't think about lawyers.

Ernie offered her dinner. "Steak and fried onion

rings? Caesar salad?"

"Nothing, thank you."

Dudley accepted the offer but said he would wait until the police had finished. He went outside to bring them in by the service entrance.

A few minutes later he was back with two plainclothes detectives. Pauline told them the entire story, including the inadequate description Rose Lipson had given of the man who took Kirby.

"And you reported that first contact to the police in your hometown?" one of the detectives asked. He was a tall man with graying hair and a dark mustache.

"Yes," she replied, "but they couldn't do anything because there was no proof of a crime. What will happen if those people find out I called you?"

"They won't know until we move in on them."

She wished she could believe it. But they even knew where to find her, and she had been so careful.

"We don't have much to go on right now," added the detective. "You just sit tight and see if they call again. Remember everything they tell you, and this is important—listen for background noises. Often that helps to identify a location. We're going to put a tap on this phone."

"Won't they know?"

"This won't be for evidence. Our main job is to get your child back safely. We'll worry about the rest of it later."

He handed her a card with his name and phone number. Richard Boyle.

They won't call again, she thought. They only wanted to shake me up. To be sure I knew they had her.

The detectives left and Dudley went out to eat his steak.

Alone, she tried to imagine a world without Kirby. What if the terrible news were to come and she knew for certain that Kirby was dead? It could happen. Even now, that moment might be waiting for her. It might really be there, in the future.

It can't happen.

She would kill herself. It was the only solution. Get some tranquilizers and a bottle of booze . . .

She jumped as a loud buzzer sounded beside her. She stared at the flashing lights on Ernie's telephone, then pressed the button for the intercom line.

Clo said, "A call for you on three."

She pushed the button marked 3. "This is Pauline Kingsley."

She could hear the tightness in her own voice, and the caller did too. His answer was smooth and mocking. "Take it easy, baby. Just keep it nice and cool."

She tried to force a calmer tone. "Yes?"

"First, lets make sure this is between you and me. You had a little time since you discovered your kid was missing. I know you wouldn't do anything dumb like call the police. Good girl. If you want to keep your kid healthy, the police stay out of it. Now, is anybody there with you?"

She looked up to see Dudley standing in the doorway. "Yes," she whispered.

"Okay, here's what you do. Tell him everything is fine. Tell him your husband came back for the kid. Got that?"

She asked hoarsely, "Jarvis?" Of course her husband was Jarvis.

"That's your cover story, lady. You're gonna stick to it if you want to see your kid again. And the kid stays where she is till either you or your husband come up with the money."

"But how—" she began.

"We'll be in touch. You stay there till you hear from me."

Dudley asked, "Was it?"

"Yes. It's okay. It was Jarvis. I mean—he picked her up at the school."

She couldn't look at him. She heard him moving toward her. He touched her shoulder.

"This is Dudley, remember?"

"I know. They told me to say that if I want to see her again."

"But they did mention seeing her again. So they took her for ransom, not for—"

"Dudley, they want the money. That's forty-six thousand dollars!"

"Well, we'll just have to see what we can do about it."

"Don't you understand? It might as well be forty-six million."

The door opened and Ernie came in. "I heard you had a call. What's the news?"

"Nothing," said Pauline. She could feel Dudley watching her. He did not expect her to keep it from Ernie.

"They said they'd call later. Don't tell anybody anything. I wasn't supposed to call the police. They told me to say Jarvis has her."

"Clo should know about it," he said.

"That's already three people. Oh God, the police." She took out the card Sergeant Boyle had given her and

111

dialed his number.

"This is Pauline Kingsley. I talked to you earlier. Yes, I just got a call. It's all right. My husband picked her up. I didn't know. I'm sorry you went to all that trouble. Yes, it's all right. And thank you."

As she hung up the phone, Dudley exploded.

"What the hell do you think you're doing? Now you've called him off the case. Are you crazy?"

"No, I had to tell them I didn't call the police. They'll know if I did. They even knew where to find me."

He conceded that they seemed to be clever.

"But I honestly don't see what choice you have. Even if we somehow manage to scrape up the money, that's no guarantee—Well, never mind."

She knew what he was saying.

"I can't think about that," she told him.

"I'm sorry, darling. And it really is up to you." He searched the desk and found a pencil and a scrap of paper. "Now, granted we don't have forty-six thousand or anywhere near it, let's think about what we do have. How much have you got in ready cash?"

"About twenty dollars."

"That's it?"

"I had to pay the school in advance for this week."

"You should definitely get a refund there. In fact, I think the school owes you a hell of a lot."

"It was my fault. I panicked. I should have gone on anyway, but I— Oh! It was this morning."

"What? What happened?"

"A car, this morning. After I left your place, I went back to the school. Just to look. I had time, and I wanted to be sure everything—was—all right." She wiped her

112

tears with the back of her hand.

"A car came by, a black limousine. Very slowly. I thought it might be following me. I couldn't see—they had tinted glass. It was like the one they came in that night, but I didn't think—I didn't see how it could be."

"Well, of course not. A lot of people have cars like that."

"Maybe I just sensed it. I should have paid attention."

"What would you have done?" he asked.

"I don't know. Maybe I would have—but I still don't understand how they knew. I only walked past. Maybe just because it was a nursery school. Dudley, what am I going to do?"

"I won't say it again, but let me just tell you this. I understand the police have a system for borrowing money from a bank for things like this, where they need a ransom. The first thing is to get the victim back safely. Then, if they can't recover the money, you're responsible, but wouldn't you rather owe the police than a loan shark?"

"Yes, but I can't. Those men are everywhere."

"Just thought I'd mention it," he said. "Now, if you can stand another comment from me, I've heard of loan sharks doing some pretty ghastly things, but not to children."

She sat with her face buried in her hands, in warm darkness. He could talk all he wanted as though Kirby were theoretical. She wasn't. She was Kirby. Pauline tried to imagine where she was now. Was she terrified? Crying? Were they treating her well? Why would they, if they meant to kill her?

Kirby, I'm sorry! I love you so much.

Would they hurt her? Would it be quick?

She lowered her hands. She had to get the money.

Dudley watched her with interest. "An idea?"

"No." She picked at a cigarette burn on the desk. "You don't have to stay here with me if you have other things to do."

"What's more important than this?" he asked.

"Well, it's just waiting, but they told me to stay here until they call again."

"What good is that if we don't have the money?"

She would offer them anything, even herself. They had suggested it.

"If we could find Jarvis," she said, "he could sign over the house."

Anne. She would try calling Anne. Would Jarvis be there yet if he had set out in his car?

No, he wouldn't. And the house had a mortgage on it, which meant the bank owned most of it. She withdrew her hand from the telephone.

Dudley said, "I've got it all figured out. We call the police, get the ransom money from them, get your daughter back, and then we sue the school."

"You still don't seem to understand. If we call the police, I won't get my daughter back."

She played it over again, the turning point. The fork in the road. She came out of Dudley's building and saw the fat man step from his car. Instead of running back inside, she ignored him and walked briskly to the corner.

The car followed her. It drove along beside her. The fat man called out, "Mrs. Kingsley!" Other people were on the sidewalk. People coming home from work. Children playing hopscotch. The inevitable stoop sitters.

The fat man, puffing in the heat, ran after her. Caught up with her. He had something over his arm. A jacket. Under the jacket was a revolver, pointed at her.

"Mrs. Kingsley, I think you'd better come with me."

She hadn't been foolish to run away. They would have gotten Kirby anyway, and her, too.

She played it again. This time, when she neared the corner and the fat man puffed toward her, she saw a police car cruising down the far side of the avenue. She screamed. They didn't hear her. She dashed out into the traffic. Brakes shrieked and horns blew. The two policemen drove on without ever knowing she was there.

An elderly man caught her elbow. "Miss, are you all right?" The fat man rushed to take her from him. "You'd better come on home, dear, you nearly bought it that time." And to the elderly gentlemen: "Thanks so much, sir. My wife—well, I really appreciate your help." And into the car she would go.

Kirby. Kirby. Kirby.

It was after eleven when Ernie came into the office. Clo hovered in the doorway while Ernie clasped Pauline's hand.

"Still didn't hear anything, huh? After that first time?"

"No, nothing."

"We're going to be closing now. Don't you want to come home and get some rest?"

"I don't see how I can," Pauline replied. "They might try to call again and this is the only number they have. Would it be all right if I just stay here?"

"Alone?"

115

"No," said Dudley, "I'm staying with her."

Ernie opened a desk drawer and showed them where he kept his spare keys. "In case something breaks and you have to go out," he said. "You never know."

"I hope you're right."

She watched them leave, down through the corridor to the service entrance. Ernie turned and called to her, "Help yourselves if you want anything to eat or drink."

"Yes. Thank you."

She went back into the office and sat down on the couch to wait.

13

Searchlights illuminated a burned-out thicket at the foot of an embankment in Steuben County, New York. Several motorists had parked their cars farther down the road and come over to watch.

"Yuck!" said a teenage girl in light blue shorts. "Was anybody in it?" Her boyfriend slipped a protective arm around her. He tried to keep her from watching as the rescue workers pried open a door and reached inside the burned car.

A wispy-haired man yelped excitedly, "There's somebody in there! All burnt up. God help him."

His wife raked the two teenagers with a dark, scathing look.

"That's what happens," she said smugly. The young people ignored her.

One of the state troopers scrambled up the embankment to his car and radioed in the license number.

"Connecticut plate," he said. "It's charred, but you can make out the numbers."

"Connecticut?" The dark-eyed woman sounded almost disappointed that it was not a local youth getting his just desserts for speeding. Who cared about some stranger passing through?

"Let's go," said the young man, trying to ease his girl away as the rescuers prepared to remove the body. He had never seen a dead body and he especially didn't want to see this one. Only last week, at a lakeside beach party, he had scorched a hot dog and watched the blackened skin flake off in brittle layers. He turned away, feeling sick to his stomach.

The girl stood fast. She wanted to watch. The wispy man, in turn, watched her. He thought she must be either disgustingly hard-boiled or a stupid, unimaginative clod.

"No ID in the car," said a young trooper, who had injured his hand while opening the still hot glove compartment. If there had been any identification on the body, it was destroyed along with the person's clothes. Impossible even to tell whether it was male or female.

He looked up at the road and the broken guardrail. Trying to go too fast around that bend, most likely. And caught fire scraping on the rocks as it fell. What people wouldn't do to save a few minutes. Or maybe the driver was drunk. Maybe an autopsy could determine that. Probably not, with the body so far gone.

"Oh, hell," he said. It was the only way he could think of to sum up his feelings. He wondered if he would ever get used to this sort of thing.

14

She had not been asleep, but the ringing of the telephone startled her.

Probably another customer. Several had called after Clo and Ernie left. She looked at her watch. It was one o'clock in the morning.

She picked up the phone. It would not be a customer at one A.M. She answered uncertainly, "Hello?"

"Yeah, Mrs. Kingsley, now listen. Go out to the phone on Park and Twenty-seventh, northeast corner. Got that?" There was a click and the line went dead.

Dudley, who had been slumped on the sofa, looked at her sleepily. "What was that?"

"I have to go out."

"Go where?" He started to pull himself upright.

"No, please. I have to go alone." She was sure of that. "They're going to call me at a phone booth. It's only a couple of blocks."

"Tricky, huh? So they can't be traced. Do you know what time it is?"

"It's okay, Dudley. I'll be all right."

"I'll expect you back in fifteen minutes," he said.

"Even if I don't come, please don't call the police."

"No, I'll go looking for you myself."

She slipped Ernie's keys into her purse and left by the service entrance.

She found the telephone with no trouble, and waited. She was surprised to discover how calm she was. Calm and ready to do whatever was necessary.

She waited, looking at her watch. How long did they think it would take her to get here?

The phone rang. She grabbed it.

"Mrs. Kingsley, now listen. You want your kid back, you're going to come up with a hundred thousand dollars."

"A hundred?"

The voice repeated, enunciating carefully, "One hundred thousand dollars."

"But I— but—"

"If you want your kid back so you can recognize her, that's the deal."

"No, wait. Where? Where do I meet you?"

Again the line had gone dead. She rattled the switchhook. All she heard was a dial tone.

He would have to call again. She waited. After ten minutes, she started back to the restaurant.

Dudley stood at the service entrance, watching for her.

"You had me worried," he said.

"They want a hundred thousand dollars. They didn't tell me when or where. I was waiting to see if they'd call again."

120

"A hundred thousand?"

"I don't know what to do."

He locked the door and they went into the office. She sat down at Ernie's desk. Dudley resumed his place on the sofa, his head back and his eyes closed, trying to think.

"They know you haven't got it," he said.

"But they have Kirby."

"So they must think you can get it from somewhere. Rich friends, maybe, or your parents."

"I don't know where my parents are. Even if I did, they don't have a hundred—" She added in her head. The motor home, the Datsun, whatever was left from the sale of their house and business.

"Jarvis's family?"

"There's only his sister. They both inherited when their parents died. Jarvis wanted the house because we were going to have Kirby, so he swapped most of his cash for Anne's share in the house, and now Anne's spent it all on men. And it wasn't anything like a hundred thousand, not in cash. There were securities, if she still has them, but it takes a while to sell those."

"How about the house? Could you sign over—"

"It's in Jarvis's name and I think he took out a mortgage."

"He could sign it over and go on paying the mortgage."

"Dudley, we'd have to find Jarvis first. And they wouldn't like it, because then they could be traced."

She took out her address book and dialed Anne's number. It was eleven-thirty in California. Anne must have been out partying. She would not be asleep. Not Anne. She could be anywhere. Spending the night with a lover.

121

Pauline hung up and rested her forehead on her hand.

"It's just hopeless. There's nobody with that kind of cash."

"Don't give up. We'll think of something. And they know you can't do anything tonight, with the banks closed, so try to get some rest."

As though she could just turn it off, like a lamp or a water faucet.

She screamed, "It's not Kirby's *fault*!"

"It never is, with that kind of thing," Dudley said. "Now, darling, I know you don't feel like sleeping, but wouldn't you be more comfortable at my place?"

"You go ahead. I'm staying here in case they call again."

"If you're staying, then I will, too."

"I'll be all right." She was exhausted. "This is probably the place Kirby remembers. Why else would they think of calling here? Besides," she added, when he still seemed undecided, "we can't leave together. I'm supposed to be in this alone."

He kissed her lightly on the cheek. "I'll see you in the morning. Or rather, later this morning."

She lay down on Ernie's couch. It was too short for her to stretch out, but it didn't matter. She could not rid herself of the ache, thinking of Kirby and what it must be like for her.

Occasionally she dozed. Then she would wake and remember that only last night Kirby had slept beside her. And the night before, they had been snuggled together in Ralph Bunche Park.

She never should have sent her to school. Kirby hadn't wanted to go. The thought of it now made her ill. She

122

had meant to start a new life for them both. She should have gotten into her car instead, with the hundred dollars and her gasoline credit cards, and headed for Florida. Anywhere. By searching enough campgrounds, she might eventually have found her parents.

She raised her head, beginning to like the idea, and then remembered that it was too late.

When morning came, she went out to the kitchen for a drink of water. It was five-thirty. Again she had barely slept. She carried her water glass into the dining room. From there she could see the street and the new day.

She remembered—when was it? Only two days ago, walking back from Ralph Bunche Park to Grand Central, enjoying the freshness of the early morning with Kirby beside her. Their own beginning ...

She must stop thinking like that.

As she turned from the window, a scrap of white near the front door caught her eye. The mail, she thought. It had come through the mail slot. But it was only six o'clock.

She went over to look at it, feeling somehow that it had to do with her. She picked it up and turned it over. On the front, clumsy block letters spelled "Mrs. Kingsly." They had put it there themselves. They must have known she was there all night. And where were they?

She held it up to the light. She could see something inside. Not paper. She wondered if she should open it, and then remembered that the police were no longer involved.

Still, she was careful to handle it as little as possible.

123

She slit it open with a dinner knife and found a lock of hair inside.

That was all. Only a lock of pink-gold hair.

She ran to the window. Two trucks and a taxi sped by down the avenue. She saw no one on the sidewalk.

Did it mean Kirby was dead? It was only hair.

"Oh, Jarvis, her pink-gold hair."

If Kirby were dead, they wouldn't tell her. Not when they wanted money. It only meant they had her.

She searched the kitchen and found a roll of plastic bags. She tore one off and slipped the envelope inside. For fingerprints, in case she needed the police sometime. Then she went back to the office and resumed her vigil.

At eight-fifteen, Ernie telephoned to ask whether anything had happened.

"No, nothing," Pauline replied, and fended off further questions. She would say nothing over the phone.

"We'll be there in a little while," he told her. "You won't be working today, will you?"

She had not thought about work.

"I guess I have to," she said. "I need the money."

A hundred thousand dollars. She would never be able to earn a hundred thousand dollars.

An hour later Clo and Ernie arrived, and soon after that came Dudley. Clo had packed Pauline's bags and brought them to her. All her clothes and Kirby's. Even Kirby's pink blanket. At the sight of the blanket, Pauline began to cry. Her emotion seemed to embarrass Clo, who quickly left the office.

Ernie put a hand on her shoulder. "Dudley says you got a call during the night. He says they upped their price."

She wiped her tears and told him what had happened.

"That means they'll have to call again," he said. "They still have to tell you where to make the contact."

"Maybe they don't," she replied, "if they know I haven't got it and can't get it."

His hand, still on her shoulder, gave a reassuring squeeze.

"Don't worry about that. Dudley and I'll see what we can do. You wait here for the phone call."

She stared at him, not quite believing it. "Do you mean that?"

"You keep quiet. I mean it. I told you I was applying for a loan, and Dudley's got certificates. Now take it easy."

They left her feeling dazed. They meant it. The whole thing might be possible after all.

Oh, Kirby!

She would work for the rest of her life to repay them both. She would do anything, as long as Kirby was safe.

She repaired her makeup and changed into her uniform. By eleven-thirty, when the first patrons arrived, she was at her station, but she found it impossible to concentrate. She mixed up another order and spilled a pitcher of water. She was hurrying to the kitchen for a forgotten salad when Clo signaled to her.

"Phone for you," Clo mouthed.

For a moment, she stood undecided. She did not know whether to take it in the office, which was more private, or at the front desk, which was closer. She reached the front desk in time to hear a click.

"Hello?" she pleaded. "*Hello?*"

Clo asked, "They hung up already?"

"They're probably afraid I'll trace the call. Oh, my

God, I wouldn't do anything. I only want Kirby back."

Clo seemed nervous. Tense and bright. She cared.

"Why don't you take the rest of the day off," she suggested, "and wait in the office. If they call again, I'll give it to you there."

When Pauline reached the office, she found Dudley there ahead of her. She had not seen him come in.

"Still working on it," he told her. "The bank says to come back later. Maybe they'll have it by then. Anything happen?"

She untied her apron and slipped it off as she told him about the call that never reached her.

He said, "I don't see how you could work out there anyway, with this on your mind. But maybe it's better to keep busy."

"It isn't. It doesn't help at all. I only wanted the money."

She sat down at Ernie's desk where a light winked on the telephone, signaling an incoming call, but not for her.

"I think they must be around here someplace," she said, "if they put that envelope through the door. I just hope they aren't where they can see in here."

"What can they see? People patting you on the shoulder? It doesn't prove we know anything."

"I keep hoping they'll call again and I can—"

"Bargain with them?"

"I have nothing to bargain. I could tell them the money's coming, so they won't—" She broke off into a sob.

"They won't," he said, emptily, because he didn't know. "Well, it wouldn't do them any good, would it?"

126

15

The Broker ran a finger under his shirt collar. It was warm in Vic's Diner. A long, hot summer, and Vic was stingy with the air conditioning.

Vic blamed it on Con Edison, the utility company.

"You know what can happen in hot weather," he maintained. "Everybody uses too much power, and something blows, and we got a black out. Or else they cut down and we got a brownout."

"Look," the Broker had told him, "I'm your partner. I want air conditioning, you give me air conditioning. If that old machine of yours don't handle it, get a new one."

From his place in a back booth, he watched Vic behind the counter, slapping together a sandwich, washing a few glasses. The diner still bore Vic's name, but he hadn't been able to control his gambling habit, and now the Broker owned half of it. Given a little more time, it would all be his. He would keep Vic on to do the work, and pay him a salary.

The Broker had always liked this diner. It made a good place to meet with clients. Its very seediness kept it from being too noticeable, but it was clean and the food wasn't bad.

He was sitting with a client now, but not really listening to what the man had to say. Defaulting on a payment was not something you could talk your way out of.

The client droned on and the Broker began to pay a little more attention.

"Yes, well, that's what I wanted to ask you about," the client was saying. "I'm trying to get the money and I promise I'll have it in just a few days, but I mean, if I can't get it, I want to know what's going to happen."

The Broker considered carefully before he answered.

"What's going to happen is, you're going to pay the money."

"Yes, but what if I can't raise that much? Let me ask you this. How much time are you willing to give me?"

"You're already overdue," the Broker replied. It had finally occurred to him that there might be something behind all these stupid, unnecessary questions.

The client looked away. "Yes, I know that, and I am trying to raise the money. Obviously, if I had a lot of money, I wouldn't have needed the loan in the first place."

"That's not my problem," said the Broker. "I loan the money, I expect it paid back."

"I certainly intend to pay it back. It's that weekly thing of yours that gets me down. It's not even interest, really."

"It's interest."

"Is that what you call it? Interest?"

"Those are all just words." The Broker studied his manicured fingernails and fleetingly reflected that it was kind of late for this man to start worrying about the terms under which he had borrowed the money.

"I don't even think it's legal," the man said. "I got a bank loan that I'm still trying to pay off. I think the interest rate there is sixteen point nine percent annually. That's a lot less than—what did you say yours is?"

"Five point—" The Broker bit off the rest of his words. This man knew damn well what the rate was, so why should he ask?

There was a record selector for a jukebox on the wall beside the table. The Broker slipped in a coin and pushed one of the buttons. He didn't care which one, as long as it made noise.

He turned back to his client with the faintest flicker of a smile.

"Five point juice," he said, as though they were having a normal conversation.

The client had seen his action with the jukebox, and heard the sound, and apparently correctly evaluated its meaning. A small worried line appeared between his eyebrows. It gave him away.

"I like music," the Broker explained with a gleam of amusement. It was a rock tune. He had heard it on the radio, but didn't know its name and didn't care.

"So do I," said the client. "Five point juice a week. I assume you mean five percent. That's a week, isn't it? Which comes to how much a year?"

"We went over all this before," the Broker replied.

"Yes, I know, but I get confused. I'm just trying to figure out how it compares with the bank."

"You like the bank's terms better, why don't you stick with the bank?"

129

The client had a rather handsome smile that appeared spontaneous, which was surprising, under the circumstances.

"They wouldn't give me another loan," he said. "I guess my credit rating doesn't look so good right now. Which brings us back to why I'm here. As we both agreed, I'm behind on my payments. I just wondered, if I can't raise the money in the next few days, I, uh—I was wondering what sort of action you're likely to take."

The Broker all but laughed. The guy was a pompous jerk who talked like a college man even when this thing could mean his life.

"What's going to happen?" he asked rhetorically, narrowing his eyes until they were slits through which he watched the man shifting nervously in his seat. "That's a tough one, isn't it? Let me put it this way. You pay what you owe, and you won't have to find out."

He hoped he had said enough, but the client looked at him grumpily. "That doesn't really answer my question."

"What sort of answer do you want? You tell me and I'll say it." By now, the Broker was enjoying himself. The music stopped and he put another coin in the machine.

"Well, I'd like to know."

"So you'll try harder to get the money? You try just as hard as you can, buddy." The Broker was ready to end the interview, but he wanted to see how far this poor slob would go.

The man leaned forward. He was wearing a light gray suit and a maroon tie. If he had a mike, it was probably under the tie or in his pocket.

"The fact remains," he said, "you can't even prove I borrowed the money. I didn't sign any papers, any agree-

130

ment. You don't have my signature on anything at all."

Again the Broker smiled.

"Who needs your signature?" he asked. "Who do I have to prove it to?" The smile grew broader when he saw his answer hit home.

He eased himself out of the booth. "Time's up, buddy. I've got somebody else waiting to see me."

As the man moved past him toward the door, the Broker muttered into his ear, "Just remember what I said. Time's up."

A man sitting at the end of the counter near the door turned to look at him. The Broker nodded toward the departing client.

The man left his half-finished coffee and followed the client outside.

16

At four o'clock, Ernie returned to the restaurant. His face was sweaty and flushed from the heat. He carried a blue canvas flight bag with fraying handles.

"There we go," he said, dropping the bag onto his desk. "They sure weren't expecting me to ask for it in cash."

Dudley went over and opened the bag. His eyes widened.

"I have never," he said, "seen anything like it."

He stood looking at it for a while, then closed the zipper. "Didn't they get suspicious when you wanted cash? They asked me a lot of questions."

Pauline shivered. She remembered that banks often reported things like that to the police.

Ernie and Dudley pooled their money, and Dudley undertook to count it.

Ernie turned to Pauline. "Did you hear anything yet?"

"Not yet. Ernie, is it really—?"

"Told you not to worry about it."

"I don't know what to say."

"Don't say anything."

I don't believe it. I don't believe it.

Footsteps clicked in the hallway. The office door was flung open and Clo came in.

She stopped at the sight of the bag on the desk. Its meaning seemed immediately apparent to her.

"What did you do?" she asked.

"I'll explain later," Ernie replied.

"I want to know."

"Okay, I'll tell you. First let me put it away." Ernie removed a calendar from the wall, disclosing what looked like the door to a safe. He turned the combination knob and the door sprang open. He stuffed the bag inside.

Clo stared after it.

"That was for us, wasn't it? That was our money."

Ernie said nothing. He locked the safe and replaced the calendar, then led Clo out to the hallway and closed the door after them.

Pauline hugged her arms to hide the shivering. How could they not call? Did it mean something had gone wrong? Had something happened to Kirby?

Dudley was speaking to her, but she didn't hear him.

"You okay?" he asked.

"No."

"They'll call. They want their money, don't they? Or I should say, Ernie's money."

"Probably they think we haven't got it."

"They'll try anyway. That's what it's all about."

Ernie's money. She couldn't feel guilty or even, at the moment, grateful. All that mattered was getting Kirby back.

133

Would she ever have Kirby back, really? Would Kirby ever be real for her again?

"It's only been a day," she said.

"That's a pretty long time in the life of a kid."

"I feel as if it's been going on forever."

"It will end. Maybe tonight."

She didn't like the word *end*.

"Then you can both come to my place," he continued. "Actually, you could even go home, once the heat's off."

Home?

In the hallway, voices rose. Then swift footsteps walked away, and Ernie came into the office. Again he was flushed, possibly from anger or embarrassment.

Dudley said, "You went and got all that money, and forgot to tell her."

"I didn't forget. I just didn't tell her."

"She couldn't begrudge it."

"No, but she's—I don't know. Touchy about money."

"She begrudges it."

"She thinks I should have talked to her first. I know I should. I didn't want problems." He shrugged.

"So now you're getting them."

Ernie went out to oversee the preparations for dinner. Pauline stood up and walked restlessly about, never taking her eyes from the phone. Its ringer had been turned off, but the lights flashed constantly for incoming calls. Clo would signal her. She waited for the buzz.

Dudley announced that he was going out to the bar. He offered Pauline a gin and tonic. A glass of wine. A beer. She refused.

"I need to relax," he told her, apologizing. "I wish you could, too, love."

134

She couldn't. And she felt that, in a way, she was doing penance for Kirby's misery as well as her own.

Ernie dropped in from time to time, offering her food and drink. She finally accepted a glass of iced tea.

When six o'clock came, she marked the time. It was exactly twenty-four hours since Kirby had been taken.

A whole day of being frightened and bewildered. Would she blame her mother? Had they drugged her?

Pauline almost hoped they had drugged her. It would dull the pain and fear.

"You've got to eat something," Ernie said when he brought her the tea.

"I can't."

"I can understand that. But it'll be okay, Pauline. At least we've got the money."

"Thank you, Ernie. I really didn't thank you enough. I don't think I can."

"It's okay."

She tried to take a sip of tea. Her body rebelled. She couldn't swallow.

"That's the bottom line," he said. "The money. That's what they want."

She nodded, and set the glass aside. "Maybe they won't let her go."

"Why not?" He rocked back and forth, shifting his weight from heel to toe. "With a kid that young, they don't need to worry about her being a witness. She won't even know where she was."

He meant well. She murmured an agreement, but she knew that his assurances were meaningless. How could he know what they would do?

"If I ever thought it would come to this—" He conti-

135

nued to rock nervously, "I'd have done what I could to bail Jarvis out in the first place. You would have been spared all this."

She forced herself to respond. "I don't know. He probably would have wasted that, too. He kept pouring money into his business. He wouldn't give up."

"It's not always easy, knowing when to give up," Ernie said. "You can't tell whether you're persevering, or plain stupid."

He was talking about himself. His restaurant. She looked up at him, and her eyes were damp.

"He was stupid," she said.

Clo could not leave her desk, and Ernie seemed to be avoiding her. It took the better part of an hour, but finally she caught his eye and beckoned to him.

He came over to the desk, smiling that foolish little half smile that was meant to turn away wrath, but only made him look sheepish.

"What if we never get it back?" she demanded. "We still have to repay it, and we'll lose everything."

"What's wrong with you, Clo? A kid's life is at stake."

"I know." And she did know. She hadn't realized it would be like this, even when they asked all those questions.

Ernie said, "Look, baby, the subject is closed. We'll worry about the money after we get the kid back."

"Don't call me 'baby'!"

"Why not?"

"I hate it. Ernie, its— we'll never get it back."

"Sure we will, if they catch them."

"They won't. I know what kind of people those are. I

136

used to run into people like that with Vic."

"I'll bet you did."

"I don't mean Vic. He wasn't like that, but sometimes when he lost, he'd have to—and sometimes they run the games, too, did you know that? They run crap games just so they can trap people."

"So what are you saying?" he asked. "That we should throw that little kid to the wolves?"

"I didn't say that."

She did not know what she was saying. It only seemed to her that people like the Kingsleys should have enough money to repay their own debts. That she should not have to be responsible for it, or forced to lose her business.

On the other hand, if the Broker didn't get his money this way, he might come back to her. So either way, it was up to Clo Fairweather to bail out the people from Connecticut who had never known what it was like to be poor.

She was still trying to figure out what to do when the telephone rang. She picked it up, and Ernie, who had started to leave, stood still and listened.

She was unprepared for the demand that came over the wire. She needed more time to think it all through.

Speaking softly, so that Ernie wouldn't hear, Clo told her caller, "She's not here. She went out."

"Went out where?"

"I don't know. She didn't say."

"When's she coming back?"

Ernie had moved in closer and was listening. He couldn't hear the voice on the phone. Only hers.

"I—don't know."

"I don't believe you, Clo. Put her on the line."

Ernie was standing over her now. Clo felt a trickle of sweat run down her back.

"She's not here. I told you."

"What are you trying to do, broad? Put her on the line."

Clo reached for the intercom buzzer. With her hand over the receiver, she looked at Ernie and said plaintively, "Is she here? I thought she went out."

Dudley came back from the bar. "How's it going?"

Pauline was still sitting at the desk. Her head ached. "How's what going?"

"Still haven't heard?"

"They won't call now. Not when the place is busy. It's just that I can't—"

The buzzer sounded. She jumped.

For her? For Ernie?

Clo's voice said, "Call on one."

"Mrs. Kingsley?" A gravelly sound. "You still keeping secrets, Mrs. Kingsley? You didn't call the police?"

"I did what you said. I told—people—it was my husband, and we've got—"

"Don't talk. Go out to the phone on Twenty-seventh and Lex. It's the northeast corner. Got that?" The line was disconnected.

"I have to go out," she told Dudley as she reached into Ernie's desk for the back door key.

"Where? Where did they say?"

"To a telephone. Just a phone. I'm going out the service entrance. Don't let anybody follow me."

"I hope this is it." He stood and watched her as she

138

walked down the corridor.

The sun was setting, casting long orange rays across Manhattan Island. Another evening. Kirby had been gone for more than a day. The pain washed through her in a terrible ache.

When she neared the telephone, she saw that it was busy. A young man in a blue corded suit stood resting his foot on an attaché case while he talked.

"No. Please, no," she said aloud. A middle-aged couple, walking past, turned to look at her.

She reached the phone and stood waiting, clenching and unclenching her hands. The young man glanced at her and went on with his conversation.

"Please," she said.

The kidnappers would get a busy signal. What would they do? Would they blame her?

The young man reached into his pocket and took out a handful of change.

"No!" she said.

He turned, glowering in surprise.

She took a step closer. "I need that phone."

He gestured toward Park Avenue and continued talking.

"You don't understand," said Pauline. "I need *that* telephone. It's very important."

He lowered the receiver. "There's two of them on the next block," he said.

Half crying, Pauline burst out, "Then you go there. I'll even give you a dime. Here. I'm expecting a call on this phone and it's a matter of life and death."

He could tell she was distraught and undoubtedly crazy. He gave her a look of disgust.

"I'm sorry," she said. "It's my child life. She's been kidnapped. Now get out of here."

He said into the telephone, "No, just a second!" The operator was cutting him off. Pauline held her hand ready to break the connection if he tried to put in another coin.

"Okay, I'll talk to you later." He hung up the phone, glared furiously at her, and strode off toward Park Avenue.

She stood by the telephone and waited. It was not really a booth, but only a sound shield. It had been easier last night when no one else was about, possibly wanting to use it. To prevent that, she had to look as though she were actually talking. She held the receiver to her ear but kept a finger on the switchhook.

What if they had tried to reach her, and couldn't and had given up? Damn the young man.

By her watch, she had waited a minute. She checked to be sure she was holding the switchhook down firmly. She rested her face against her hand and wanted to cry, but she couldn't.

Another minute. How could they blame her if the phone had been in use? It was a public one, after all. How could they take it out on Kirby. She was only four years old. A baby who still sucked her thumb when she slept, and needed a pink blanket. A baby.

Another minute.

She should have stayed in Allenbury. Should have taken them up on their first idea and become a hooker. She would have been enslaved, hooking forever just to pay them their weekly interest, without a chance of getting rid of the loan itself, but even that would be better than this. At least Kirby would be alive and taken care of.

Another minute. She ceased to have any thoughts at all. Suddenly the telephone rang.

"Mrs. Kingsley?"

"Yes, I'm sorry. There was a—"

"Do you have the money, Mrs. Kingsley?"

"Yes."

"You got it? All of it?" He sounded surprised. They would know she couldn't have gotten it by herself. They would know she had help, and therefore must have told someone.

Not the police. I didn't get it from the police.

"Yes," she said. "All of it."

"Okay, here's what you do. Now listen good, I'm only going to say this once. You put the money in a suitcase or some kind of bag that shuts tight, a lock or a zipper. You take it over to the train tracks on West Forty-fourth Street. You know where the tracks are?"

"The subway?"

"I'm talking about the railroad. It's an old freight line between Tenth and Eleventh Avenues. On the north side where the bridge goes over, there's a break in the fence. West side of the bridge. It's big enough so you can go through, and there's a path that goes on in. There's trees and bushes on both sides. On the left side as you go in, the side away from the tracks, put it under the first bunch of trees. Make sure it don't show from the outside. That's twelve o'clock midnight tonight and nobody goes with you. Got that? Okay, Mrs. Kingsley."

"Will—" she began. *Will my child be there?* But he had hung up.

17

At eleven-thirty, she left the restaurant. She carried the bag of money and went out alone, in case they were watching her.

Five minutes later, Ernie left, too. They met at the garage two blocks away where Dudley kept his car. He waited for them across the street.

Pauline got in beside Dudley, and Ernie next to her.

"Do you know the place?" she asked.

"I know where the tracks are," Dudley replied as he pulled away from the curb. "I take my car around there for servicing, and when I go to pick it up, I walk over the tracks. You wouldn't notice them if you weren't on foot. They're way down."

"Down from what?"

"From the street level. It's sort of like a canyon. You don't have to leave it on the tracks, do you?"

"No, there's a place. He told me where."

She felt herself beginning to shiver again. Squeezed into the front seat between the two men, she tried to hide it. She watched the city glide past her and remembered that she had told Kirby it was pretty at night, and they would enjoy it together. They hadn't had a chance.

Would they ever have the chance? She folded over as a wave of nausea attacked her.

"It makes a certain amount of sense," Dudley said. "There's practically nothing but repair shops around there, and they'd all be closed at night. Except for the Hess station on the corner, but I don't think they could see, not on the north side."

Ernie noticed that she was hunched over. "You okay?"

"I'm scared," she said.

"All you have to do is put it there, right?"

"I'm scared it won't work."

Dudley said sharply, "Don't think like that."

"I don't trust them." She hugged the money bag on her lap. "I don't see how they can torture a child. What kind of people could do a thing like that?"

He braked suddenly as a light turned red. "Is that what they threatened?"

"They said something about getting her back so I can recognize her."

"It's a bluff. Don't think about it."

He drove along Forty-second Street and up Eighth Avenue. At Forty-fifth he turned west again, then drove half a block down Ninth Avenue and parked.

"Okay?" he asked. "We should be out of sight here. Unless you want one of us to go with you part of the way."

"No, I don't. They might be watching me."

Ernie got out of the car and reached in to help her with the bag.

143

"Are you sure you'll be all right? Walking around in the middle of the night with all that?"

"Nobody will know what it is," she said. Her teeth began to chatter. "If anybody tries to take it, I'll scream."

"We'll listen for you. It's not the greatest neighborhood." Ernie got back into the car and she started off.

Although traffic moved up and down the avenues, the side streets, lined with small brick and brownstone buildings, were nearly empty of cars and pedestrians. A nighttime desert. The only thing real about any of it was the feel of her feet on the pavement. The soft night air against her face.

The block was a long one, dim, quiet, and nearly deserted. She kept her senses tuned in all directions for anyone following or approaching her. In the distance, the twenty-four-hour Hess gasoline station was a bright oasis of light.

She had never traveled through this area on foot before, only driven past it. She had thought all the freight tracks were underground. What if she couldn't find it?

She turned in alarm at the sound of footsteps somewhere behind her. It was a man walking alone with his head bent forward. She quickened her own pace, and when she looked back again, the man was climbing a flight of steps into one of the buildings.

She reached Tenth Avenue and stood on the corner waiting for the light to change. She could not see the tracks. During a break in the traffic, she hurried across the street.

North side, he had said. She was on the north side. She looked for a bridge, and there wasn't one. Suddenly she was crossing a deep ravine and the tracks were at the

144

bottom of it.

She looked about for a waiting car. They must be somewhere around, watching her. Beyond the tracks was a fenced-in playground. It was probably closed at night, all playgrounds were, but she saw a group of boys playing basketball inside.

West side of the tracks. North and west. It was a chain link fence and she saw the hole in it. There were trees inside. An odd little woodland in the city.

She crouched down and stepped through the hole. As the man had said, a path ran along the embankment, disappearing among the trees. She avoided a dog dropping. It was not only children who had made the path.

A clump of trees. For a moment, she panicked. Had he said right or left? The first clump on the left. Her mind was racing. He had said bunch, not clump. On the left as you enter the path. They were sumac or ailanthus. She couldn't tell the difference. She tucked the bag under them. It was still plainly visible.

But they had told her what time to leave it. They would be along to pick it up almost immediately. Before morning, when the dog walkers came. But what about the drug addicts and the lovers? She pushed the bag closer to a tree truck and backed away before someone could see her.

She started to leave, then went back once more to be sure the bag was secure. After a final check, she ducked out through the fence to the sidewalk.

Again she looked around at the shadows, the parked cars. Perhaps it was too much to hope that they would be there with Kirby. They would wait until they had the money, and they would count it, and then they would let her know. Maybe. She had done her part.

Half walking, half running, she returned to where the car was parked. As she rounded the corner on Ninth Avenue, she looked back to see that no one had followed her.

Ernie climbed out so she could get in. As she took her place beside him, Dudley gave her a hug.

"Any sign of them?" he asked.

"I didn't see anybody."

"They'll probably pick it up later." Dudley started the engine. "Then they'll call you about releasing the kid."

"Please. I don't want to talk about it." She felt as though the shivering would begin again, but she was only drained.

18

They would pick up the money. Then they would call her. She waited at Ernie's desk for their call. From time to time she rested her head on her arms. Once she dozed and dreamed of her childhood.

She woke up when the telephone rang.

"Mrs. Kingsley?"

That familiar voice. This time—

"Mrs. Kingsley, where's the money?"

She noticed that the room was growing light. Had last night been part of her dream?

"I put it where you told me." A chill crept over her as she wondered whether she had gotten the instructions wrong.

"On Forty-fourth Street," she added, to be sure. "Just off Tenth—"

The phone clicked.

"Wait!"

She could not believe it. Waves of hot and cold washed through her as she sat watching the room fill with daylight.

It wasn't true.

She needed someone. Anyone. She reached to call Dudley's number, then withdrew her hand.

She did not know whether to leave the telephone or wait. But the waiting would drive her mad. She took her purse and the back door key and went out to the corner, where there was a pay phone.

After she dropped in her dime, she wondered if they might be watching.

If they were watching her, she thought bitterly, they would have known where she put the money. She dialed.

He answered with a sleepy "Huh?" She looked at her watch. It was not quite six.

"I'm sorry." Her throat tightened and she began to cry.

"Pauline! What is it?"

"They just called. They said the money wasn't there."

After a moment, Dudley muttered, "Damn."

"I'm sorry. I don't know what to do."

"That's not— Oh, hell."

"I thought I had it right."

"You couldn't make a mistake with that. Unless they forgot what they told you. Maybe we should go and have a look. I'll pick you up in—twenty minutes?"

"Oh, Dudley."

"I'll call the garage right now. Wait for me at the service entrance."

She waited inside the door, keeping it ajar so she could see when Dudley arrived. When he did, she slipped out quickly and got into the car.

He hadn't even shaved. She brushed her fingers across his cheek. "Thank you."

"It's okay. I wish I could do more than this."

148

"You and Ernie are doing everything."

"Yeah." A bitter agreement, because it hadn't paid off.

The traffic was light at that hour and they reached the west side in a few minutes. He drove up Tenth Avenue and parked at Forty-third Street.

"In case they happen to be around somewhere," he said. "This whole thing might be a trap. Do you want me to go and look?"

"I'll go. If they're anywhere near here, they shouldn't see you at all." She got out of the car and hurried up the street. She didn't think it was a trap. Only a mistake. The bag would be there—

The bag was not there. She could see it wasn't, even before she climbed through the fence. She groped under the trees to be sure, then pulled aside other branches and leaves. She walked part way along the path, and peered down at the tracks. There was debris on the tracks, but nothing that looked like the blue canvas bag.

It was gone. The bag was gone. She felt her legs weaken under her. She clutched at the fence, then climbed through the hole and went back to the car.

"It isn't there," she told Dudley. "Somebody must have picked it up. How could they? Who even knew it was there?"

A *hundred thousand dollars. Kirby's life.*

"Maybe somebody saw you put it there," he suggested.

"I looked. I'd have noticed somebody watching me."

She was going to be sick. Or black out.

"From inside a car?" he asked. "Maybe it was a derelict or someone just poking around."

"What am I going to do?"

149

"Maybe the kidnappers got it and they're lying."

"No. No, I could tell. What am I going to do?"

"Do you think people like that are honorable?"

"Dudley, it wasn't that. Somebody picked it up. I should have stayed."

"Don't be silly. You weren't supposed to stay. We just assumed they'd be right there to get it."

"They'll kill her now."

"You told them you put it there."

"But they didn't get it! Oh, my God, they'll kill her!"

"Take it easy."

"How can I?"

He put his arm around her. She rested her head on his shoulder and felt him stiffen.

"It was all you had," she said. "You and Ernie."

"Money can be replaced."

Oh, Kirby. Kirby, I tried.

There must be something more she could do. Something she could have done differently.

Dudley said, "I know it won't help, but would you care for some breakfast?"

She couldn't think of eating.

"I'm terribly afraid I need some coffee," he apologized. "Would you mind?"

She barely heard him, but it didn't matter. He started the car and cruised until he found an early morning coffee shop.

"You're sure?" he asked.

"I'm sure. I'll stay in the car."

"Good. I probably can't park here anyway." He patted her hand. "Sorry to abandon you, but if I don't have coffee, the brain won't function. Besides, I get a headache.

150

And don't give up, darling."

Don't give up. She had heard him say it before, or maybe it was Ernie. *Don't give up.*

Why not?

A truck drove in behind her and blew its horn. They wanted her to move. She slid across the seat and started the car.

She drove around the block. When she returned, Dudley was still inside the coffee shop. She began to weave back and forth along the streets. If she could find something, anything—someplace where they might be holding Kirby....

It was a stupid idea. She could not tell anything from the street. Every few minutes she passed the coffee shop to see whether Dudley was waiting.

When she finally picked him up, he asked, "Did you get any bright ideas? Is that what you were doing?"

"No, but I'd better get back to the restaurant. They just might call again."

"You did try," he said.

"I don't think that counts."

No one else was there yet when they returned to the restaurant. They let themselves in through the service entrance and went to the office.

"I've got to find Jarvis," she said.

"How?"

"I'm going to call the house. Just in case. And then Anne."

She dialed her home telephone number and heard the announcement she had recorded. She waited through the entire message, on the very small chance that Jarvis might be there and would pick up the phone.

There was no answer. She did not know what to do. It was barely eight in the morning. Inez Collins was probably asleep. It was possible, just possible, that Jarvis might have tried to get in touch with her, Pauline, and failing that, might have called Inez to check on her.

As soon as Inez answered the phone, Pauline knew she was up and already drinking.

"Jarvis?" asked Inez in bewilderment. "Didn't you find him?"

Pauline remembered her story about Jarvis being in the hospital.

"No, Inez, that wasn't true. Jarvis ran away. I don't know where he is, but I've got to find him, it's very important. I wondered if you might have heard from him."

"From Jarvis? No, honey, I don't know about Jarvis, but some policemen were over at your house. They were looking for you."

"Police? For me?"

"At your house. They couldn't find you and they came to see me. I told them you went away. I said you had your little girl in the car—"

"What did they want me for?"

"I remember your little girl in the front seat, with that little playsuit she wears."

"Inez—"

"You told me to watch the house, but I didn't know where you went."

"Inez, the police. What did they want?"

"They were looking for you. I said you went—"

"Did they tell you *why* they were looking for me?"

"Oh . . . it was about Jarvis. You said he was in an accident."

152

"But that was—"

"That's it." Inez seemed pleased that she could remember. "That's why they came. It was the accident. Oh, wait a minute."

"Inez, what did they *say*?"

"Well, they wanted to know where you were. Because of Jarvis."

"What about him? Please!"

"It was something about the car. It caught on fire, I think."

"Oh, my God."

"They said— No, wait a minute. It was Jarvis's car. Oh, honey, I'm so glad you're all right."

"A fire?" It was not the accident she had invented for Inez. It was a real one. "Did he get hurt?"

"Oh, he's dead."

Dead. She murmured, "Thank you," and lowered the phone.

Dead.

Her hand was shaking as she dialed Directory Assistance in Connecticut. The Allenbury police. Wherever it happened, the police in his hometown would have been notified.

It wasn't true. Another dream. Their pound of flesh. She knew. They used to read it together. Shakespeare. *Oh, Jarvis.*

The Allenbury police had been trying to find her. It had happened in New York State, somewhere in the vast western part. She had never heard of the place. The car was established as his and they wanted the name of his dentist so they could check the records. It wouldn't do any good, her going to identify the—

She clapped her hand over her mouth.

They were still talking to her. They wanted her to go back to Allenbury.

"I can't," she said, and hung up the phone.

She had forgotten about Dudley until then.

"Jarvis is dead," she told him.

19

The two younger Rodriguez boys had gone to watch a ball game in the street outside their apartment. Twelve-year-old Billy had pleaded a stomach ache. "Maybe later," he told his brothers with a realistic groan. "You go on. Go ahead."

They hadn't wanted to leave without him, but he insisted. Finally he was alone. His small bedroom was dim and shadowy with the window shades pulled down to keep out the sun. He pushed the door partway closed. Not all the way. That would look suspicious.

Kneeling by his cot, he reached under it and pulled out the bag. As soon as his hand touched the rough canvas, he started getting dizzy. This much of it, anyway, was real. For a while that morning, he hadn't been sure. And the stomach ache was real, too. His insides felt the way they did on the first day of school, all nervous and blown up with excitement and a little bit of fear.

Now would come the test. He would find out whether the rest of it was true, or whether the lights at night had played a trick on him, or he had dreamed the whole thing. He tugged at the zipper. It resisted at first, and then gave. And Billy stared, with butterflies inside him and his head reeling, and he still thought something must be wrong.

It was funny money. It had to be. Counterfeit, or play money from some kind of game. It looked real, but nobody would put real money under a tree by the railroad tracks.

The money was in packets. He lifted out a few and riffled through them. Twenties. Fifties. Hundred-dollar bills. He had never seen a fifty- or a hundred-dollar bill before, and here were bundles of them. It was unbelievable. It didn't make sense.

He wondered how long it would take to count the whole thing. There must have been a million bucks in there. A million bucks of funny money. He might be wasting his time, but he couldn't get over how real it looked.

A hundred. Two. Three. Four. There was a thousand dollars right there in his hand. A whole thousand.

He stopped and listened. Somebody was coming. He flipped his rumpled bedsheet over the bag, but he wasn't fast enough. Angel, his young stepfather, stood in the doorway.

"What have you got there?" Angel asked.

"Nothing."

"I saw you with something. What is it? You started dealing?" Angel came into the room. He was going to pick Billy up by the ear and thrash him for dealing drugs, and it wasn't fair.

Still, the money couldn't be real anyway, so maybe it

156

didn't matter if Angel knew about it. Shit.

"Just some bag I found," Billy replied, and pulled back the sheet.

"You found it?" Angel did not believe him. He still thought it was drugs. "Let's see what's in there."

"It ain't what you think. It's just some paper."

"Paper!" Angel's eyes popped and he nearly fell into the bag. He reached for the top bundle, the one Billy had been counting. The hundred dollar bills.

"It ain't real money," Billy told him.

"Who says so?"

"I do. It can't be."

Angel was reaching in with both hands, stirring the money around, trying to see what there was. He cursed and muttered to himself. He couldn't believe it. Neither could Billy.

"Hey, kid— Kid, what did you do, knock off a bank?"

"I found it," Billy said again.

Angel hooted.

"I did. I saw a lady put it under a tree, and I went to see what it was."

"A tree? Where?"

"By the tracks. You know that place."

"What lady?"

"How the hell do I know? Just some dame."

"A real—?"

Billy realized that Angel thought it must be a miracle, and he laughed.

Chagrined, Angel demanded, "Why would anybody do that for?"

"How do I know? Maybe *she* knocked off a bank."

"We got to put it somewhere. It ain't safe."

157

"The hell! It's mine, I found it."

"You're crazy, kid. All this?"

"You can't— I'll cut you in, okay?" It was a desperate plea. Billy knew his stepfather would probably take all of it.

Angel was starting to say something when they heard her voice.

"What's going on there, fighting again?"

It was Jenny, his wife. Billy's mother. She pushed open the door and looked in, a handsome, dark-haired woman, years older than her husband. Angel flushed a deep red because sometimes she treated him like one of her children, and she was doing it now.

"What's happening?"

Angel sat on the cot, with the bag hidden behind him.

"Nothing. Why do you always think something's happening?"

"Because it is. I could hear you. What did you do, find some money?"

"Couple of bucks."

"You wouldn't fight like that over a couple of bucks. What was it, a lot?"

They did not reply.

"If it's a lot, and you don't know who lost it, you should take it to the police."

"I ain't going to no police," Angel said.

"It's not right—"

At that moment, the baby, who had been running a fever, began to wail. Hearing the fretful cries, Jenny forgot about the money and went to look after her child.

When they were sure she had gone, Angel swung the bag down onto the floor where they could hide it more

158

quickly the next time.

But it couldn't stay there. If it was anywhere in the apartment, Jenny would find it.

"We got to put it somewhere," Angel said again.

20

Kirby. And then Jarvis. It couldn't have happened. Only a few days ago, they had been a family.

It made her sick, thinking of how he had died. It was exactly the sort of thing they would do. But why? It must have happened before the money was lost. Even before she had left it by the tracks. So why had they done it?

"It doesn't matter why," Dudley told her. "That's the kind of people they are."

"It means they followed him. And me, too. You can't get away from them."

She thought about it now, in the afternoon, alone in Ernie's office. At that time of day there were scarcely any customers, and Dudley had gone out to join Ernie and Clo in the dining room.

Maybe it really was an accident, and not a pound of flesh. That meant the debt was still unpaid. And they would not let Kirby go because they hadn't gotten their money.

She couldn't think. She felt suspended in time and space.

The buzzer sounded, shocking her. She picked up the phone.

"Call on two," Clo said.

A woman's voice asked, "Is this Paulette Kingsley?"

"Pauline. Yes."

"I have some information about your daughter, Mrs. Kingsley. If you're interested, I want you to be out at the side door of that restaurant in ten minutes, and I want you to be alone. And you'd better not tell anybody, okay? Is anyone there now?"

"Who are you?" Pauline asked.

"I don't want any questions." The woman hung up.

Pauline looked at her watch. It was five minutes to four.

A woman had been there when Kirby was kidnapped. The same one? Now she was willing to talk. Ratting on the others, most likely. She would want money, and Pauline had none to give her.

Or else it was a trap. They were going to kill her because she hadn't paid them.

She looked at her watch again. Less than thirty seconds had passed. She wanted to go out and tell Dudley, but they might know if she did. They seemed to know everything.

She could not sit still. Ten minutes . . .

The door opened and Dudley came in.

"Darling, you haven't had anything to eat or drink. You should at least take liquids. It's very important. Something to do with your trace mineral balance."

He didn't ask about the phone call. Was it possible that Clo hadn't mentioned it?

"I'm all right," she said. "I might even go out for a while."

161

"I thought you couldn't leave the phone."

"I don't think they'll call. It's been hours."

"Do you want me to go along?"

"No. No, I have to think. I'm in shock. I just want to think about everything."

"Right," he said.

"You go on back and—do whatever you were doing."

Dudley caught on, and leaned back his head in a nod of understanding.

"I hope this is it," he said.

"I don't know, but please don't say anything. And don't try—"

"I won't. I didn't hear anything and I don't know anything. I'll get out of your way now, love, and good luck."

She hadn't time to thank him before he was gone.

Five more minutes. She hoped the woman would understand that she had no money. She must understand. Probably none of them believed she had ever had the ransom money or tried to pay it.

After eight minutes, she went to wait at the service entrance. She counted the seconds. At exactly five after four, a dark gray car with tinted glass windows drew up to the curb.

It was the same car that had waited for her two days ago outside Dudley's building. When the back door was opened, she caught a glimpse of male knees in a gray suit.

It was the fat man. He must have intercepted the woman who had called. He beckoned her inside.

She hesitated. But they still had Kirby, and there was nothing else she could do. She climbed in beside him.

"Mrs. Kingsley." He reached across her to pull the

162

door closed, and the car began to move.

They were going to kill her.

She tried to explain. "I really did put the money there. Right where you told me. I went over to look this morning after you called and it was gone. Somebody must have found it and taken it."

He waved his hand dismissively.

"We're not talking about that. That's not why we're here, but of course it's unfortunate if the money disappeared. Naturally I have no way of knowing whether you're telling the truth."

"But I—"

"I'm going to give you one more chance, Mrs. Kingsley. One more chance to see your kid again. I'm going to make a deal with you."

He paused to watch the effect. She said nothing. She wouldn't tell him there was no money left.

"One more chance," he repeated. "There's something you can do for us. I'll see if I can explain it."

She glanced out at the city, which looked oddly golden through the tinted glass. And then back at the man. She couldn't meet his eyes, and didn't want to.

"The first thing you're going to do," he said, "is get in your car and drive back to that house of yours in Connecticut. You still have the car, don't you?"

"It's in Connecticut. But I can get it, if it hasn't been towed away."

He regarded her silently.

She said, "I left it in a parking lot. I'm sure I can get it."

"Yes. And you'll go back to your house and act like nothing happened."

"How can I?" And then, with dawning joy: "Will I have my daughter?"

"Not till it's finished. You just go there like nothing happened. Like before."

"It can't be like before. My husband is dead. I just found out. And the woman next door knows about it."

"Yeah?" said the man. She watched him closely to see if he knew about it, too. She couldn't tell.

"You go there," he said, "and do whatever you have to do. But don't say nothing about this part of it, understand? You say your daughter's visiting her aunt, whatever you have to. Got that? And you wait for a phone call. You'll know when it comes because somebody will tell you. And you just act natural, like nothing happened, and do whatever they tell you on the phone. Got that?"

She nodded.

He said, "When you get that phone call, you play along and keep us posted, or you can forget you ever had a kid. Do I make myself clear? Now where's your car?"

"It's in North Port. Connecticut. I could get there by train, but I have no money. I'm completely broke."

"How much is the train?"

He gave her two ten-dollar bills. More than enough. She was not even to go back to Ernie's restaurant. They drove her to Grand Central Station and let her out at the Park Avenue entrance.

It was close to rush hour and the station was already filling with commuters. She walked through the waiting room, remembering her time there with Kirby.

She mustn't remember. Mustn't think. Just do as she was told.

She bought a one-way ticket to North Port. They told

her the next train was already boarding. She found the gate and started down the ramp toward the platform, remembering Kirby's complaints when they first arrived.

Mustn't remember.

She kept her head down in case any of her friends or acquaintances happened to be on the train. She found a seat next to the window and sat looking out at the tunnel, remembering—

The train trip took an hour and ten minutes. She felt as though she had gone back in time when she stepped off at North Port into the hot, late-day sunshine.

At the A & P parking lot she found her car where she had left it. The tires were chalk-marked, indicating that she had overparked. She opened all the doors and windows to let out the heat, and then began the drive home.

Long roads with rich green lawns, secluded estates, a riding stable or two. She drove out of her way to avoid the main part of Allenbury. Then she was on Dogwood Road, with its split levels and fake Tudors.

With mounting excitement, she approached her own house. The excitement turned to dread as she entered the driveway. Dread of what was to come. With her remote control, she opened the garage doors and drove quickly inside before Inez could see her car. She could not cope with Inez or anyone. Not even Sue Rhinehart.

From the garage, she unlocked the door into her kitchen. Her beautiful kitchen. The entire house was hot and stuffy with air that felt long dead. It was a tomb. A memorial. It made her ache with sadness.

She started to open a window, but it didn't matter. What was there to save electricity for? She went into the living room and turned on the air conditioner.

165

She searched the entire house, not quite certain as to what she was looking for. Perhaps to be sure it was all right. Not that it mattered. The only thing that mattered—

The telephone. She was to receive a call. She went into the den and shut off the answering machine.

The den, with its large antique desk, reminded her of Jarvis. She sat down at the desk and began opening its drawers. She must acquaint herself with all the things that were here, all the household business. A packet of unpaid bills. A folder labeled "Taxes." The remote key for the answering machine.

The remote key. She hadn't seen it when she looked before. It was here. All the time it was here. So they hadn't found her through Dudley's message. There was something else . . . She couldn't think. It was like a pain, nagging her, but she couldn't think.

She played the messages on the machine. Dudley's call. Sue Rhinehart: "We're home from Mystic! Where are you?" The mother of one of Kirby's friends, wanting Kirby to come and play. Sears Roebuck, trying to sell her a service contract on the washer.

Jarvis. And Jarvis again, his voice living on.

He had called. He had tried several times to reach her. If she had waited . . .

But she couldn't. There hadn't been time.

Perhaps they had followed him and he needed help. What could she have done? She couldn't do anything. Her whole family was gone now.

She raised her head and listened. A sound. In the kitchen? The back door. It might have been Inez, but Inez usually came to the front door because it was closer to

166

her house.

She got up and went out to the living room. She was frightened now.

Could it be? she wondered. Could it be that the police report was wrong?

Footsteps scraped on the kitchen floor. They were coming toward her. And then, in the dining room door-way, loomed the shape of a man.

She screamed.

21

He grinned at her. The thin man with the bald head. He began to laugh.

"I see I got company," he said.

"How did you get in?" Pauline demanded.

"There's ways of getting in everywhere."

"Is this part of it? Did they tell you to do this?"

"Sure." He stood looking her up and down, as the fat man had done on that first night. Then, she had been wearing shorts. Today she wore a flowered wrap skirt and a cotton knit shirt.

"If you're in on it," she said, "then maybe you can tell me what's supposed to happen now."

"You wait for the call."

"What call?"

Instead of answering, he disappeared once more into the kitchen. She heard the refrigerator door open, then the pop of a flip top. Jarvis's beer. She felt as though Jarvis were being violated.

She started toward the stairs, to get away from the

168

man. But the beds were upstairs. It might be too sugges-
tive. Instead she went into the den. If the call came, she
could take it there.

She stood at the window, looking out at green rhodo-
dendron leaves. Why should they call her here? Why not
give her the message, whatever it was, in New York?

It must have something to do with the house. They
wanted her to do something. Burn it and turn the insur-
ance money over to them.

She would do it. Anything, if they would guarantee
Kirby's safety.

This time she did not hear him approach. The carpet
deadened the sound of his feet, but she knew when he
was there.

"Getting tired of waiting?" he asked.

"No." The one-syllable answer came out with a qua-
ver. She wanted to say more, to establish her confidence
and authority, but the less she communicated with him,
the better. She turned away and looked out of the win-
dow again.

"You scared of me?" he asked.

"Why should I be scared?"

"Maybe you're just a snob."

For a moment, she forgot her position.

"If you want to know, you're not the first thing on my
mind. My baby's been kidnapped, my husband's been
killed, and you expect me to concern myself with you?"

His face drew together angrily.

"That's not too smart, talking like that. I can take care
of your kid, you know."

Again she refused to answer. She must not become
embroiled. She rested her forehead against the window

and knew she was leaving a smudge. After a while she heard the whisper of his feet, walking away.

She had intended to spend most of her evening in the den, but she was not free of him there. He came in to watch a baseball game on the best and biggest television set. She went out to the living room and tried to read, but was unable to concentrate. She curled in an armchair and closed her eyes.

She woke suddenly as something touched her. He was standing in front of her, pressing his legs against her knees.

She recoiled. He bent down and pinned her shoulders to the back of the chair.

"You better be nice to me," he said.

Kirby.

"Come over to that there couch."

If it had to be, it had to be. She got out of the chair and went to the sofa. He untied her wrap skirt and fumbled with her underclothes. She gritted her teeth, forcing herself to think only of Kirby.

"You better be nice to me, bitch," he slobbered into her ear. "You better be nice or your kid's gonna get it."

She felt him against her bare skin. Smelled the beer on his breath. Then suddenly, with a curse, he slapped her and got up from the sofa.

She pulled on her clothes and looked around at the windows, hoping no one had been able to see in. She gagged at the thought of what might have happened. Thank God for Jarvis's beer. It must have made him impotent. She settled back in the chair, reflecting bitterly that Jarvis took better care of her in death than he had in life.

170

In the morning, she woke before the man did. She saw him lying on the couch in the den, still sodden from the beer he couldn't hold.

She took a shower, keeping it brief so she could finish before he woke up, and made herself a cup of instant coffee.

Halfway through the coffee, her stomach turned over in a spasm of nervous fear. There had been no call. Had they changed their minds? What would happen to Kirby?

Please let this be over with. Please. Let me get her back safely. It's not her fault.

She heard him grunting in the den as he woke. He called, "Hey, bitch!"

"I have a name," she said as she went to him. Would this be a repetition of last night? Would he please brush his teeth or wash his mouth first?

He sat up on the couch and patted the cushion beside him. "Come over here."

As she started toward him, the telephone rang.

She looked to him for instructions. He pointed toward the phone. She was to answer. She picked it up.

The fat man's voice said, "Mrs. Kingsley? Put him on."

She held it out to him. He spoke briefly. "No, nothin'. I been here all night. Nothin' yet. Yeah, okay."

He stood up unsteadily. "I gotta take a leak."

"There's a bathroom next to the kitchen."

"If you get a call," he instructed her, "just act normal and do everything they say."

She heard water running and the toilet flush. He must have left the door open.

The call was still expected and it wasn't from the fat

man. She felt the nervousness again. The tightness in her chest. She must keep her wits about her. Act normal and do as the caller said.

The man was crashing in the kitchen when the phone rang again. She heard the thump of running footsteps. Saw him fill the den doorway as she picked up the receiver. And then she forgot him.

"Paulie, you came back!"

"*Jarvis? Jarvis, is that—you?*"

"Who else?"

"But you— they told me— they said you were dead."

"Yeah, I heard about that."

"How did you—"

A piece of paper was thrust in front of her. On it the man had scrawled clumsily: *Ac normle. Do lik he ses.*

Oh, dear God. This was the call.

Her mind went blank, and she groped for what she had been saying. A question.

"Are you hurt? Where are you?"

"I'm not hurt. I wasn't in the car. It got stolen. I'm in New York."

"Where?"

"At a hotel."

"Why? Why can't you come home?"

"There are reasons. I have to talk to you. I left you in an awful mess, Paulie. Has anybody— Have you been bothered at all? Oh, hell, I can't talk over the phone. I want to see you. Can you bring Kirby and come here?"

"Why can't—"

The note. *Do lik he ses.* She didn't understand it. Something was happening.

"Kirby's not here," she said. "She's staying with some-

172

body. I—thought it would be better. But I'll come. Where are you?"

"I can't tell you where I am, but here's what you do. Take the train into the city. What's today, Saturday? Just a minute."

She heard the rustle of paper. He must have had a timetable.

"Take the twelve-forty train. There'll be somebody waiting for you at the gate."

"Jarvis, what—"

"Don't ask. We can talk about it when you get here. As I said, somebody will meet you at the train gate in Grand Central."

"How will I know who it is?"

"You won't. He'll know you. I'll show him your picture. Then he'll take you to where I am."

She didn't like the sound of it. "Is everything all right?"

"Everything's fine. I'll see you this afternoon. Are you sure Kirby's okay?"

"Yes. Why?"

"Can she stay there overnight, with her friend?"

"That's what she's been doing."

"Good. It's better. Don't forget, the twelve-forty train."

The thin man stood in front of her with his arms folded.

"So what's the story?" he asked.

"I'm supposed to—"

She had to stop and think. Jarvis couldn't be with them. Or maybe he was. This man did not know what Jarvis had said, but the call was important and she was to do what Jarvis told her.

"I'm supposed to take a train."

"Yeah?"

To get Kirby back, she must tell him what he wanted to know, and do as he said.

"The twelve-forty train. Somebody's going to meet me in Grand Central."

"He's going to meet you in Grand Central?"

"Not him. Somebody. Somebody I don't know."

She seemed to be saying the right things. The thin man looked pleased.

"And?" he prodded.

"And that person will take me to where my husband is."

The man broke into a wide smile.

"You're doing good, bitch. That's just about right."

22

It was over lunch at the Emerald Bar & Grill that Detective Sergeant Dick Boyle first heard about the bag of money.

"Ninety-eight thousand dollars." Rocky O'Rourke emptied half a bottle of ketchup onto his roast beef sandwich. "Can you believe that woman giving up ninety-eight grand? It wasn't even hot. Nobody knew she had it. I thought her husband was going to kill her."

"Maybe he will," said Dick, rescuing what was left of the ketchup. "It's funny, you know? You hear a thing like that, and you can't help feeling the person is some kind of sucker, or maybe a nut. It's a shame to think that way. She's one in a million, but, hell, I wonder why she did it."

"Said she thought it was the right thing."

"She's incredible. There should be more people like that. Only trouble is, you just get trampled. Nobody ever thanks you. Did you thank her?"

"I guess so. I was kind of stunned."

Dick took a swallow of coffee. It burned his mouth. He

had been thinking so hard, he forgot it was still hot.

"Where'd she find it?" he asked.

"Her kid picked it up. She heard the kid and the husband arguing about it. She didn't know exactly where—"

"Will you find this kid for me?"

"For you? What for?"

"I don't know. It's just a hunch. I didn't hear of any robbery, did you?"

"It's not even your precinct," Rocky pointed out.

"A hundred thousand, man. If that much was stolen, it would be all over the media."

"So what do you think?"

"I think it might be ransom money."

"Any particular reason?"

"I don't know. I don't know if it has any connection at all. It's just a feeling I get. There was this case a few days ago...."

Pauline drove back along the same quiet roads she had taken the day before, past lush greenery and prosperous homes. Yesterday it had seemed unreal, something long past, because Jarvis was dead. Today he was alive.

"How did you find him?" she asked the thin man, who sat beside her in the car.

"Huh?"

"My husband. How did you find him? By tracking, or an informant?"

The thin man was in control now, directing everything she did. It gave him a smooth confidence.

"We didn't find your old man, lady. That's where you come in."

"What do you mean?"

"He found you. Right?"

And now she was to lead them to him. That was why she had been sent home. She was the only one who could do it.

They must have known he would call her. That he had been trying to reach her. The messages on the answering machine. And he was in hiding. Was that where he had been all along?

He couldn't meet her at the station. Someone else would be there. Someone who was helping him, who didn't know Pauline.

Oh, Jarvis! She was beginning to understand. *Jarvis, your friends, they didn't tell you about Kirby!*

Because they didn't know.

"He doesn't know about our daughter," she said. "That—that she's—"

She drove through an intersection. Her eyes saw the other car, but her brain failed to note it. Her ears heard the shriek of brakes, the angry blare of a horn.

"Don't stop," said the man.

She hadn't thought of stopping. The running of the stop sign, the near collision, had nothing to do with her.

"All you have to do is tell him about our daughter. He won't do anything then."

"Yeah? How do I tell him?"

Oh, God. She was to lead them to him.

"I'll tell him," she said. "He'll get the money somehow. He'll do anything to keep her safe. We both will."

She was on the outskirts of North Port now, guiding the car with numb hands. Numb because they were shaking. Always shaking. A quivering wreck. If she were stronger and smarter, she could have planned her way

177

out of this right from the start.

Today she parked at the station. She remembered the other time, carefully choosing the A & P parking lot so they wouldn't follow her. And still they had found her.

The man stood to one side while she bought two round-trip tickets to the city. He had told her to buy round-trip, as though they were a suburban couple going into town for the day. He had given her the money.

As they stood on the platform waiting for the train, she asked, "What's going to happen after you find him?"

"That's up to you," he said.

"What do you mean?"

"Not here. I'll tell you when we get on the train."

The words chilled her. "When we get on the train." That was so she couldn't change her mind about going to Jarvis. It was something terrible that they planned to do.

But how could she change her mind? She was trapped. They had Kirby.

In the distance, the train tooted. She watched it roll into the station.

They boarded and sat together. He would not let her out of his sight. When the train began to move, he reached into his pocket.

"You see this?"

She looked down at the bottle he held half-concealed in the curve of his hand. A prescription bottle, with a blue and white label and a glass stopper.

"Yes, I see it."

"You're going to take this. I'm putting it in your handbag. You be careful it don't break, understand?" He opened her purse, which was resting on her lap, and

178

slipped the bottle inside.

"What is it?" she asked.

"You don't have to know. You go to that place where your husband is, and then you break it."

"What?"

"You dumb or something? I said take it to the place—"

"You said to break it. What is it?"

"I told you, that's not your problem."

They wanted her to kill him. Her. Pauline. To kill Jarvis.

"Why?" she asked.

"Because if you don't, there's going to be one less kid in the world."

"I mean—my husband. And why me? What's happening?"

He hesitated as though considering whether or not to tell her. Then he said, "I don't know what you're talking about."

She was only supposed to follow orders. Not to ask. It was Kirby or Jarvis. They left it up to her. Kirby or Jarvis.

She turned toward the window. At first she saw nothing. After a while, as the trees and buildings sped past, she remembered that other trip, only a few days ago. She had been happy then. Yes, happy. She hadn't quite realized it at the time.

She had to go back. There must be some way she could get back to that day.

But the train rattled on, and the thin man, instead of Kirby, was beside her. And she had to choose. Kirby's life or Jarvis's. Why hadn't he died in that accident?

Kirby, she thought. Kirby, who was blameless. *But how can I do this? My own husband.*

179

"Please tell me what's in the bottle."

"Damn it, quit asking," he said.

"I want to know. Can't you let me have that much? I want to know what's going to happen."

"Lady, you want your kid back? Just do like I told you."

"How?"

"Throw it. Hard. Throw it so you break it. If it don't break, step on it."

"What will happen to me?"

"You'll be okay."

"But—"

What would happen? Was it poison gas? An explosive?

Kirby's life. She must think of that. Only Kirby. She would have to smash the bottle the first time, because if she were close enough to step on it—

Kirby. Think of Kirby.

"What if I can't go through with it?"

"That's your tough luck." He sounded bored. "It's going to be tough on your kid."

"I don't see how you can do that to a child. None of what happened is her fault."

"So?"

"Do you have children?" she asked.

"None of your business, bitch."

He seemed asexual to her, in spite of last night.

"Don't you have anybody you love? Do you have any feelings at all?"

"That's got nothin' to do with it."

She supposed it didn't. He might have had feelings of his own, but not for humankind or for life in general. If he had children, he did not identify them with Kirby. He had no ability to empathize.

180

"Tell me something," she said. "If I do what you want, do you guarantee I'll get my daughter back?"

"That's the deal, ain't it?"

"That's what he said. Your friend. But I have to be sure. You know what you're asking, don't you? It's going to take all I've got. Maybe more. And then I'll have to live with it. So I've got to know that—that I'm getting my child back and everything will be over."

"If that's what my buddy said, you can count on it."

The thin man sat looking down at the floor. She thought there was a faint crinkle at the corner of his eye.

23

The boy refused to talk.

"I don't know nothin'," he replied to Rocky O'Rourke's questioning, when he bothered to answer at all. His eyes, evading Rocky's, were full of anger.

"Bill, I understand where you're coming from." Rocky reached for the boy's arm to get his attention. Billy shrugged away the hand.

"You had all that money, that incredible amount of money that you found," Rocky continued, "and they took it away from you. That's enough to make anybody mad."

"I found it," Billy said sullenly. "I didn't take it from nobody. I thought if you found it, you got to keep it. That's what I heard."

"It's not exactly as simple as that," Rocky explained. "Your mother did the right thing, even though it seems unreasonable to you. We keep it for a while and try to find out who it belongs to. If we don't find the owner, then it's yours."

182

"Yeah?" Billy showed a glimmer of interest.

"That's right. We have to give the owner a chance. How would you like it if you lost some money, a lot of money, and nobody gave you a chance to get it back?"

"I dunno." Clearly Billy had no sympathy for anybody who could afford to throw around a hundred thousand dollars.

"Well, that's how it is," said Rocky. "Deep down, you knew it was too good to be true, didn't you? Well, it was. The thing is, you might still have a chance. You play fair with us and we'll play fair with you. What do you say?"

"I dunno." Billy rested his chair on two legs and gazed over Rocky's head at a crack in the wall. He had never been inside a police station before. He was unimpressed.

"So what do you want from me?" he asked.

"I want to know exactly where you found the money."

"Uh—I found it—uh—over by the river."

"Where by the river?"

"The docks. Where the boats are. There's like a wall."

"Was it near the wall?"

"No, it was—it was back a little ways. It was down where the Circle Line dock is. There was a trash can. Like a dumper. One of them small-size dumpers. That's where I found it."

"Are you in the habit of looking through garbage dumpsters?"

"Yeah, why not?"

"Lucky you," said Rocky. "You hit the jackpot."

Kirby had fallen down the stairs and her mother wouldn't come to help her. She lay in a heap with her arms twisted painfully under her. She couldn't move and she could not cry out.

When her eyes opened and she saw the darkness, she knew it had been a dream. But still she couldn't move and her arm ached.

Now she remembered. They had tied her hands. She lay on a hard bed and she must have rolled onto her back. She whimpered and tried to move, to get the arms out from under her. There was something stuffed in her mouth. A piece of cloth.

She could see the room now. It was a dim, dark basement with one small window way above her that was half covered by a piece of wood.

Voices were talking somewhere out of sight.

"Train gets in—forty-eight. You figure—"

They didn't live in the house. She remembered the house when they first brought her here. It was empty and dusty and all the windows were broken.

It was hot, too. She couldn't breathe. She tried to spit the thing out of her mouth, but it was too big. In panic, she rolled her head from side to side.

She heard footsteps, and looked up frightened. He stood next to the bed, watching her. The man with the face like a plate. The shiny-haired woman was beside him. Kirby whimpered again, trying to force the rag from her mouth.

The man turned away. The woman folded her arms and smiled. It was not a nice smile.

"You know why that's there?" she said. "Because we don't like to hear kids yelling."

Kirby wanted to tell them she wouldn't yell, but the thing kept her from talking. She wouldn't yell if only they would let her breathe.

184

"Don't worry about it, kid," said the woman. "It's not too much longer. In a little while your mom and dad will be going bye-bye and then you can go, too."

Her own parents never talked babytalk to her, but she knew what it meant. The woman's nasty smile told her she would never see them again. That she would never get away from here.

She saw the face grinning down at her, and then it was gone in a blur of tears.

Rocky O'Rourke shifted in his chair. He hated to sit for any length of time, but at the rate the kid was going, it might be all day.

"Okay, Billy, how about the truth this time?"

Billy glowered. "That's the truth, man!"

"No, it isn't. I got enough from your parents."

The kid clammed up again.

"Listen," said Rocky, "this could be very important."

With a sullen shrug, Billy replied, "So, somebody ripped off a bank. What the hell, banks got a lot of money."

Rocky squared his shoulders. Banks, insurance companies, department stores. It all ended up with the little guy paying, and he was a little guy.

"It's not banks that have the money," he said, "it's people. It all comes from people like your mother and father, who put their money in a bank to keep it safe. That's whose money it is.

"Anyhow," he went on, leaning forward, which caused Billy to back away from him, "I don't think it's that. Nobody'd rip off a bank and then put the money where a kid like you could find it. That just wouldn't happen. I

185

think it's something else, and I think somebody's life may depend on it. Now I want to know where you found it. And no more stories, Bill. You're talking to a guy who's already heard part of it."

Another shrug. "If you know, then why are you asking me?"

"I want the details." Rocky added desperately, "Look, you'll probably get a reward no matter what happens."

That news seemed to appeal to Billy, who brightened for perhaps the first time since he had come.

"Okay, I found it on the tracks," he said. "Not on the tracks, it was way up high. See, you go where the tracks are, Forty-fourth Street, and there's this hole in the fence . . ."

Rocky listened and memorized. He did not want to rattle the kid by taking notes.

"You saw a woman put it there," he said, "or put something there. Can you tell me what she looked like?"

"I dunno. It was night, see. And I was pretty far away. She had on a—like a skirt and a white thing on top."

"Was she thin? Fat? Short?"

"Sort of—I dunno. Maybe tall. Not too thin. She was built."

Rocky looked down at the written description Boyle had given him of Pauline Kingsley. She had been sitting down most of the time Dick saw her, but he mentioned her figure. And her height. A woman who would catch your eye.

"What about her hair?"

"Uh—I guess it was dark. Yeah, dark. Down to here." Billy indicated his shoulder blades.

It was not much to go on, but it did not rule out Pauline Kingsley.

186

24

The train pulled to a stop in Grand Central Terminal. Pauline sat in her seat, unable to move.

I can't do this.

The thin man jolted her elbow. "Get going, baby. This is it. Remember, it's up to you, what happens to your kid."

I can't.

It was Jarvis or Kirby. She would have to choose. Kirby or Jarvis. How could they do this to her?

She was scarcely aware of getting up from her seat. The thin man guided her down the aisle and out the door to the platform.

Jarvis had done this. He had gotten them into it. If she could remember that, and be angry ... But she had no more strength to be angry.

They were marching in a solid herd, all the passengers, toward the train gate. She heard a whisper in her ear. "Act natural." Then she was alone. He had dropped back so they would not be seen together.

Help me. Please help me.

The ramp leveled and she walked through the gate. She slowed her pace but did not look around. Maybe no one would be there to meet her. She hoped. She prayed. They couldn't blame her for that, if there was no one to lead her to Jarvis. They couldn't blame Kirby—

Someone cried, "Pauline!"

A woman? One of her friends? What a time to run into one of her friends!

A young woman with dark hair and glasses rushed toward her, threw her arms around her.

"Pauline, how great to see you!"

She tried to draw back. The arms clutched her tightly. The woman murmured, "Come on, I'm an old friend. Play it up a little."

Pauline tried to smile. "So nice to see you." She felt as though she would break.

"What's the matter, a bad trip?"

"It was—" She couldn't see the thin man, but knew he was there, somewhere behind her. She could tell the woman everything. He might not hear her, but he would know if the plan went awry. It meant Kirby's life. As long as they had Kirby, they had Pauline, too.

"It was okay." She could not manage any more.

The woman led her across the main concourse and up a flight of stairs to the Vanderbilt Avenue exit. There they encountered a line of taxis depositing and picking up passengers.

"Frank's going to meet us here," the woman said loudly. "Remember Frank?"

"Oh, yes."

Pauline was not doing very well. She couldn't think of talking. The few words she did say meant nothing. She

188

was disembodied from her voice, from her feet. A green car stopped beside them and the driver said, "Hi, how are you?" They walked around to the passenger side. Pauline slid in beside the driver. The woman got in next to her and closed the door.

"I guess this is all pretty strange to you," said the woman as they waited for the light at Forty-second Street, "but you really should play along with us in case anybody's watching. You never know. I might have been followed, or you might have. Jarvis will explain it to you."

Pauline said hoarsely, "I think I figured out some of it."

In the rear-view mirror, she could see a yellow taxi in back of their car.

"But who are you?" she asked. "How did you get into this?"

"We're police officers."

"What?"

The woman smiled. "You sound as if you don't like the idea, but it's okay. We're just trying to keep Jarvis safe. He's a valuable witness."

"Oh, my God," Pauline breathed.

"He'll be all right. We know what we're doing."

In Vic's Diner, just below East Fourteenth Street, a man sat in his usual place at the counter, near the door and not far from the telephone. In front of him was the usual cup of tepid coffee. A prop. After it started to cool, he rarely drank it.

Vic rang up some change on the cash register. As far as Vic knew, it was just an ordinary Saturday.

"Is the Broker coming in today?" he asked the man,

189

whose name was Nero.

Nero stirred his coffee and answered with a shrug. He really didn't know. Usually it was his job to be there in case the Broker needed him, when the Broker was meeting with a client. Today was different. He had to wait for a phone call, and when it came, he was to cross the street to the abandoned building where Ruby kept guard over the kid. The building was marked to be torn down and there were no phone connections in it. All communications had to come through Vic.

"More coffee?" asked Vic. "Hot it up for you?"

Nero looked at his watch. There might be time to eat something.

"Gimme a sandwich," he said. "Ham on rye. And when Tommy calls, that's for me. It's important."

"Tommy's going to call here?"

"That's what I said."

As Vic went to make the sandwich, Nero glanced out of the window at the building across the street. He couldn't stop looking at it, watching to see if there was anybody, namely a cop, snooping around. It was his job to safeguard this part of the operation. He didn't like to think about what would happen to him if anything went wrong.

Inside the building, Ruby watched through one of the broken windows. He, too, was looking for cops, or anything that might screw this up for the Broker. It was a pain in the butt having to keep the kid alive all this time, but she was their insurance. It wouldn't be much longer, though. As soon as Nero notified him that the call had come, he and Barb would take care of the kid once and for all. They had a plastic trash bag, three-mil strength,

190

all ready for her.

From where he watched, Ruby could see inside the diner. He saw Vic turn from the grill and reach under the counter, where he kept the telephone. Ruby leaned forward, tense and alert.

Vic held the receiver to his ear and slapped some hamburgers onto the grill with his other hand. At the sound of Clo's voice, he turned to mush. He had never gotten over her.

"Hey, baby, it's good to hear—" he began, but Clo interrupted.

"Shut up and listen to me." She was speaking in a low voice, and the harsh breathiness hurt his ear.

"Tell Ruby the cops are here. It's not my fault, just tell him. That woman must have blabbed to her husband that she was here and it got to the cops."

Vic looked up to see Nero watching him. Nero could hear his end of the conversation, but probably could not hear Clo.

"Yeah?" Vic said into the phone. "What do you want?"

"I said tell Ruby, you jerk. He should get away from there. Get rid of the evidence."

Although he hadn't seen it, Vic knew what the evidence was. He had been sending over food for the little girl.

"Will do," he replied. "Yeah, yeah. Right."

25

Frank brought the car to a halt in front of the Madison Motor Inn. Pauline and the policewoman climbed out and Frank drove away.

"Right in here," said the woman, heading toward a door that slid open automatically. As it closed after them, Pauline looked back and saw a yellow taxi pull up to the curb.

The thin man. He would be there to know if she followed his instructions. Or if she didn't.

In the elevator, she began to feel sick. The woman mustn't know. She clenched her teeth and tried to keep her face calm. Stealthily she reached into her purse. The bottle was still there.

I could tell her, she thought. If she's a policewoman, I could tell her.

She took a breath to tell the woman about Kirby but no words came out. There would not be time to rescue Kirby. The thin man would be listening, waiting for an explosion. If it didn't come, Kirby would be dead before the police ever found her.

The elevator stopped. She thought it was the sixth floor. Her head was spinning and she could barely see. She felt as though she did not belong to her body. The door opened and they floated out into a carpeted hallway.

"Pretty nice accommodations, don't you think?" the woman asked. "Shows you how important he is."

Pauline did not know what she was talking about.

They stopped in front of a door marked 612 and the woman knocked. There was no guard at the door. Pauline had thought there would be a guard. Maybe inside the room with Jarvis. But when the door was opened, she saw that the room was very small and only Jarvis was there.

The policewoman said something Pauline did not hear, and then was gone. Jarvis, in chino slacks and an unfamiliar shirt, locked the door. It had three locks. Then he turned to her smiling, and took her in his arms. "Paulie, honey, you're here. I was afraid you wouldn't come."

She hated the name Paulie. The last time he had held her was after their fight, when he was going out to buy beer. It was the last time she had seen him. She could not remember how long ago it was.

"Look," he said, "I didn't think— I thought I could just get away and that would be the end of it. I wanted to tell you—"

She couldn't hear the words. He mind had shut itself off. She stopped being aware of him until he held her at arm's length and gently shook her.

"You're like a piece of wood. What's the matter?"

She imagined the bottle breaking and flames exploding into the room. She saw Jarvis, all on fire, trying to stumble his way out.

"I've been in a state ever since, worrying about you and the kid. I kept trying to call you. I was afraid they got to you."

"I was at Ernie's," she said.

"Ernie—Hampden?"

"I couldn't find anybody else."

"Pauline, I have to tell you—"

"They've got Kirby. They took her from the school. They wanted money and Ernie got the money, but it never—"

"Ernie what? He got the money? What money?"

"He borrowed some money. He was going to renovate his place. But he gave it to me, to get Kirby back. I put the money where they said, but they never got it. They told me I have one more chance." She reached into her purse and took out the bottle.

"It's this. For you. It's my last chance to get Kirby back."

His eyebrows drew into a puzzled frown and he stared at the bottle, trying to put it all together.

She said, "I can't do it, Jarvis. And Kirby will die."

"What is it?"

"I don't know. They wouldn't tell me. They said to throw it so it breaks."

"An explosive?" He took the bottle from her. She had not really looked at it before. It was filled with a clear liquid.

"Nitro?" he asked. She didn't know. He said. "I think it's meant for both of us."

194

"What do you mean?"

"Paulie, look. They want me out of the way so I can't testify. Do you think they want you around to testify?"

"I don't know. I can't think. Jarvis, we have to do something. There's a man downstairs. He came with me. He said—they said they'd let Kirby go if I—"

The thin man didn't really care about Kirby. None of them did. She knew it, but did not want to know it.

"We have to do something," she said. "And Jarvis—they found me. After I came to the city. I was trying to get away from them, but they found me. I thought they traced me through a phone call. I thought they had the remote key, but it's in your desk, so they couldn't—"

"You were at Ernie's, you said."

"Yes, but Ernie wouldn't—"

"No, not Ernie. At least, I don't think he would."

"Clo?"

It all tumbled together. Clo knew where she was, knew where Kirby was going to school, and had asked very sweetly that Wednesday afternoon if she had "found the friend she was looking for." Meaning Dudley. She had even managed to find out where he lived.

"Clo," said Jarvis, "is the one who told me about the Broker."

"Who's the Broker?"

"The loan shark."

"Oh, my God."

"Paulie, I came back. I kept calling home, but you weren't there. I didn't know where you went."

"Only the people who weren't supposed to know where I went knew where I went," she said bitterly.

"After my car got stolen, I went to the police. They

195

sent me back here. I told them everything, and then I had to go meet with the Broker and carry a microphone."

She put her hands over her face. Jarvis, impractical Jarvis, had had more courage than she did.

"But I think the Broker guessed, so the police put me up here—"

"And then they got me," she said. "They got me to find you and— Jarvis, we have to do something. We can—as long as he gets what he's waiting for."

"Blow up the hotel?"

"It's not enough to blow up a hotel. But we have to do something. To get some time."

"What about Kirby?" he asked.

"I don't know. We have to find her."

"I'm going to call them." He sat down next to the phone on the night table.

"Call who?"

"The police."

"Don't let them do anything! They said they'd kill her if we told the police."

He lowered the phone. "The police don't know?"

"I couldn't. They said they'd kill her."

"We have to, Pauline. How else are we going to find her?"

"But they—" She was beginning to shake again. "They said they'd let her go, after—"

"And you believe that?"

No. No, she really didn't.

"But he's waiting," she said. "He's here, waiting."

"Who?"

"The man. The one who followed me. I saw a taxi—"

196

"Where is he?"

"I don't know. But we can—we can fake it. I figured out how. We can turn the bed on its side and hide behind it, and throw it into the bathroom. If it's a firebomb, we can slam the bathroom shut. If it explodes, it might blow out the wall and we can go in the next room."

"Why the next room?" Jarvis asked

"In case the man's waiting in the hallway. He might kill us if he sees us, and they'd kill Kirby, too. We have to make them think we're dead."

"What does the man look like?"

"He's thin, with a thin face and a bald head. He's wearing black pants and a pink short-sleeved shirt with a black and white necktie."

"Sounds distinctive, anyway." Again Jarvis picked up the phone. He dialed, and then he was talking. Telling the police what he had learned from her.

"We're going to fake it," he said into the phone. "We don't know what will happen. Now listen, go and check out Uncle Ernie's Steak House on Lexington Avenue." He gave the address. "There's a woman named Clo. Do whatever you have to do. Strangle her, but make her talk. It's our kid's life."

Pauline searched for escape routes, in case her plan didn't work. They were too high to jump. She opened a door. The closet with bare wire coat hangers. It left only the bathroom.

"What's your room number?" she asked.

"Six-twelve. Why?"

"And the one over there, on the bathroom side?"

"Six-fourteen."

She dialed the motel operator and asked for room 614.

197

She did not know what she would say if anyone answered. No one did.

"It's empty, at least for now," she reported.

Together they turned the bed on its side near the wall away from the bathroom. They crouched behind it. She glanced at the door, three locks. What if it was a firebomb? How would they ever be able to open the door?

"Get down," he told her.

Aiming carefully, he flung the bottle at the far bathroom wall.

Tommy had put a jacket on over his pink shirt, and a toupee on his head. He didn't trust anybody, not even a bitch whose kid was in danger. He had bought a copy of the *New York Post* and sat in the motel lobby, pretending to read.

That bitch was taking one hell of a long time. Probably she couldn't handle it, but she had to think of her kid. It was one or the other. One hell of a fix. He had rarely had so much fun in all his life.

Then he heard it. A loud thud.

Was that it? She did it!

He stood up. People rushed past him. Some bolted out to the sidewalk. Others sprinted for the stairs and the elevators. Wisely, he avoided the elevator and ran up the stairs. He didn't know which floor it was. He went up, up, wheezing for breath. He lost count, and then he saw a hallway where a crowd had gathered. He saw pieces of rubble. A man came toward the stairs, motioning everyone back.

"Alla you, get away from here. We don't know what happened, we don't know how stable it is. Come on,

198

folks, you can watch it on the news."

Tommy slipped past him. He did not know which room they had been in, but most of the damage seemed to be around 612 and 614. He tried the door of 614. It was locked.

Someone took hold of his arm. "You gotta move out of the way, sir. Gotta leave room for the emergency teams."

He had wanted to be sure, but they wouldn't let him stay. He went back down the stairs, hearing sirens. They were closing in fast. By the time he reached the lobby, several police cars and a fire truck had arrived. He headed toward a bank of pay phones. Every one of them was occupied.

"Shit," he said. All those people wanting to talk about it. Maybe reporters calling in.

He ran out to the sidewalk, dodging firemen. Had to get to a phone. Let them know. He had done a good job. The phone call was part of it. If anything got screwed up, the Broker would nail him to the wall.

He chugged down the block, looking for a phone. The pay phone on the corner was busy. He had been running so hard, up all those stairs, he thought he was going to black out.

On the next block, he saw a cigar store. He plunged inside. Two phones, and one was free. An old woman, halfway down the narrow aisle, waddled toward it. He elbowed past her and got there first.

26

Dick Boyle spotted the green car as an unmarked police vehicle.

He was leaving Ernie's Steak House in frustration. The woman had simply disappeared. He had her address and phone number in Connecticut. For lack of anything better, he would try there.

He had one foot in his own car when the green one swooped in from a side street and double parked next to the restaurant. The man and woman who got out of it seemed in a hurry. Too much of a hurry for lunch, even a late lunch.

He stopped them as they were about to enter the restaurant. They tried to push past him. A big hurry. He identified himself.

"I'm on a kidnapping," he said. "The Kingsley case."

They were stonily silent. He was about to berate them for professional jealousy, when the woman said, "Come on in. I think we've got a lead."

The Fairweather woman looked up and saw him. She

hadn't expected him to come back in. Her face seemed pale.

In a low voice, the female police officer asked him, "Is there a woman named Clo?"

"That's her," said Dick.

The two officers presented their identification. Frank Novak and Dorothy Arno.

"You were the one," Arno said to Clo, "who steered Jarvis Kingsley to a loan shark called the Broker. We want to know where to find the Broker, and we want to know fast. A child's life is in danger."

Clo opened her mouth. It took a moment for the words to come out. "I don't know—where—"

"Can the funny stuff," Arno snapped. "If you steered Kingsley, you must have told him how to reach the Broker."

"Why don't you ask him?" Clo replied.

"Damn it!"

Arno had a temper. Her partner put his hand on her arm.

It was mid-afternnon and the restauraut was almost empty. Ernie Hampden noticed the cluster around Clo's desk, including Boyle, whom he knew by now, and went over to see what was happening.

"The Broker," Arno was insisting. "The loan shark. Do you want to be responsible for a kid's death?"

"I don't have anything to do with it," Clo insisted.

"Withholding vital information," said Frank Novak.

Ernie asked, "What information?"

Arno pounced on him. "Do you know anything about a loan shark called the Broker?"

Ernie looked baffled. Dick Boyle said, "These officers

201

have information that Miss Fairweather was the one who steered Jarvis Kingsley to the Broker. Finding the Broker is our only hope of saving the kid."

Ernie's blankness turned to shock. He looked at Clo, who stared back at him defiantly. Dick groaned to himself. A family confrontation was not what they needed right now.

"You can talk about it later," he said. "We've got to find the Broker."

"I don't know any Broker," said Clo. She sounded less sure of herself. They probably could have worn her down, but there wasn't time.

Ernie said. "You told me you used to run into people like that with Vic. He'd know, wouldn't he?"

"Vic," said Arno, trying to keep them on the track.

"Runs a diner," Ernie supplied. "Vic's Diner. It's down around Fourteenth Street. He'd probably know."

Clo wiped a tear, smudging her eye makeup.

"That's where—people go to meet the Broker. He's there in the afternoon, a lot of times. I don't"—she sobbed—"know any other place. If somebody wants to see him, they"—another sob—"they ask Vic when he's going to be there. Oh, Ernie!"

In Vic's Diner, the telephone rang again. Nero leaned forward to listen as Vic reached under the counter.

"Yeah," said Vic into the phone.

"Gimme Nero."

Vic recognized Tommy's voice. They had told him the call would be important. Naturally they didn't bother explaining. From what Clo had said, and the way these guys were behaving, he thought he could figure it out.

"He ain't here right now," Vic replied. "Probably back in a few minutes. Want to leave a message?"

There was a pause. No one expected Nero to be out. Vic heard a muttered "Shit," just before Tommy hung up.

Nero watched him suspiciously. "What was that?"

"Nothing," said Vic, as he busied himself wiping the counter.

"Was that for me?"

"You ain't the only guy in the world."

Nero spent enough time in the diner to know who did and who did not receive phone calls there.

His lips stretched across his teeth. "You creep, was that for me?"

"If it was for you, I'd give it to you, wouldn't I?" Vic rinsed out the rag and wiped the counter again.

Nero slid off his stool. "You creep."

Vic had three customers. He saw three faces watching in alarm.

He hadn't a chance behind the counter. He stepped out in front of it. Nero reached under his jacket. Vic smashed a fist into his jaw.

Nero sprawled on the floor. He rolled over and started to get up. Blood trickled from his mouth as he reached again for his shoulder holster. Vic kicked him in the head.

A woman screamed, "Help, police!" The customers scrambled for the back door. Through the window, Vic saw one of the women stop at a pay phone outside.

The police car rocked, its tires shrieking, as it careened around a corner onto Fourteenth Street. Pauline was

203

flung against her husband.

"I thought I wanted to kill you. Before. Before they gave me that."

"I really never imagined—" Jarvis began. He didn't have to finish. It was the fiftieth time he had said it. "They could have had the house, the business, anything," he went on. "I just didn't know."

She was not interested in apologies. She knew it would be too late. Kirby could be anywhere. Brooklyn. New Jersey. They would kill her and throw her into the harbor.

Dick Boyle's driver swerved around a truck. Dick was on the radio, trying to reach whoever was in charge.

"Tell 'em to have all units move in quietly. *Quietly.* No uniforms up front. Park the squad cars out of sight. This is a kid's life."

The kick in the head had stunned Nero for a moment. Just a moment, but Vic had gotten the gun and was pointing it at him. Vic reached for the telephone. He would get the police. If they could come without being noticed, there might be a chance.

"You're crazy, man," said Nero.

"I know it," Vic replied.

He wasn't sure what he was doing. He knew it was no way to treat the Broker and his men. It would mean the end of him. They would probably torture him before they killed him, but better he than a little kid. A little girl. He'd always wanted kids....

It wasn't easy, dialing with one hand. He should have had pushbuttons. He got in a couple of digits before he heard the siren.

204

Damn hell, that woman customer of his must have called the police. And there was Ruby over in that house with the little kid, hearing sirens.

"You gotta stay quiet," he said to Nero. It was useless. Nero laughed. Vic put his finger on the trigger. He didn't know how to fire the thing. What if he missed?

The sound of the siren filled the air. He twirled the gun in his hand and brought the butt of it down on Nero's head. The guy could take anything. Vic beat him a few times, until he was down on the floor, and then rushed out into the street.

27

Vic had not yet reached the abandoned house when the front door opened and Ruby came out.

He prayed that Ruby hadn't seen him scuffling with Nero inside the diner.

"The cops are coming," he gasped, hunching over as though to clutch at a stitch in his side. He was hiding the gun, Nero's gun, under his apron.

"Get in here!" Ruby grabbed his arm, hauled him inside and closed the door.

He was in. And so far Ruby didn't suspect anything. Vic looked down to be sure the gun was still hidden. If only he knew how to work it. He didn't dare try. Ruby would be much faster.

The platinum blonde named Barb was there, her blue eyes huge and alarmed. Ruby hustled them both down a flight of stairs. It was a black pit. Vic could see nothing. His eyes had not adjusted from the bright daylight. He stumbled on a step. In a moment of panic, he imagined falling and dropping the gun. He reached out blindly to catch himself. A railing, thank God. He felt the splinters pierce his hand.

"Over there." Ruby pushed him and again he stumbled. In the darkness he heard a rustling sound and then a whimper.

A child's whimper. The little kid.

The darkness started to clear and he could see a few shapes. He saw Ruby doing something over by a bed. Looked like he was untying something. The child began to sob. She sounded exhausted. Hopeless.

"You," Ruby said to Barb, "get over here. You're going to carry this kid."

"Carry—?" Barb asked.

"We're getting out of here."

"What about me?" asked Vic.

"Who the hell cares about you?"

He could see a little better. He saw them start up the stairs. They would get away, taking the kid with them as a shield. As soon as they were safe, they would get rid of her.

He had sent food over. He hadn't fed her for nothing. And he always wanted a kid.

On a side street, the police car pulled over and stopped.

"What's happening?" asked Pauline.

"Gotta stay out of sight," said the driver.

Jarvis leaned forward. "Is she here? Is that what they said?"

"Nobody knows. They only know the guys usually meet around some diner here."

Pauline covered her face. If only she could hide there in the blackness. Hide forever and have none of this be real. It couldn't be real. Her whole life had been a dream.

Jarvis said, "A minute ago, I heard sirens."

"Yeah, that was a unit coming in response to another call."

"My God, I hope they didn't—"

Somewhere in the distance, a voice blasted through a bullhorn. Pauline gave a little scream and huddled further into the darkness.

She heard Jarvis ask, "What's happening?"

The car radio crackled and the officer started the engine. They were moving out into the street. They rounded a corner and she saw what looked like a sea of policemen and cars.

"How can they do this?" she cried.

Nobody heard her. The two officers in the front seat got out of the car.

And then she saw it. Kirby, in someone's arms. A woman with silver-blond hair. And walking directly behind her, with his arm reaching around to point a gun at Kirby, the fat man.

"Kirby!" she cried, pushing open the car door.

She heard Jarvis call, "Pauline!"

A policeman blocked her way. "Stand back, ma'am. He's got a gun."

"But that's my child!"

"We're doing everything we can."

Which was nothing. There was nothing they could do. She saw the couple inching toward a parked car. She saw a crowd of policemen standing helplessly. She heard the bullhorn again. They were asking the fat man to talk to them.

It wouldn't work. Not with the fat man. He knew ex-

208

actly what he was doing. He had nothing to talk about.
Something moved in an open doorway. A man in
white. A cook, or something. She heard a shifting among
the policemen. The blond woman stopped walking and
the gun edged closer to Kirby's face.

The man in white was not far behind them. He walked
bent over as if something were hurting him. Pauline
barely paid attention. Her eyes were on Kirby, and she
held her breath.

She caught only a flash of white as the man moved
suddenly. The blond woman screamed. Then Kirby was
on the ground and the police were rushing toward them.

"Kirby!" she cried as the child was passed to her.
When Kirby was in her arms, she had a sudden, fleeting
sensation that this was the moment she had lived for all
her life.

Then it passed, and Kirby was hugging her and crying
and Pauline cried, too. And Jarvis hugged them both.

In the distance, she saw the man in white surrounded
by policemen. She tried to move closer to him and
couldn't.

"What happened?" she asked. "What did he do?"

One of the policemen said, "He slugged the guy. Had
a gun under his apron. He used the butt. That's some
arm."

Another added, "He knocked the guy's gun hand out
of the way."

"Who is he?" Pauline asked.

"Think his name's Vic," someone said. "He runs that
diner over there."

"Clo's ex-husband," Jarvis explained to her. "He's a
gambler."

Pauline stared at the man who had saved her child's life.

"Whatever he is, this time he won. I hope they give him a medal for it."

Jarvis's arm tightened around her shoulder. "You deserve a medal, too."

"For what?"

"For everything."

She rested her head against his. Kirby was squeezing her neck.

"It doesn't matter. It's all over. I can't believe it's all over and I have my family back."

"Not quite over," he reminded her. "We still have to testify."

"That," said Pauline, "will be a pleasure."